Dirty Rush

Dirty Rush

A NOVEL

TAYLOR BELL

G GALLERY BOOKS

New York London Toronto Sydney New Delhi

G

Gallery Books
A Division of Simon & Schuster, Inc.
1230 Avenue of the Americas
New York, NY 10020

First Gallery Books trade paperback edition January 2015

GALLERY BOOKS and colophon are registered trademarks of Simon & Schuster, Inc.

For information about special discounts for bulk purchases, please contact Simon & Schuster Special Sales at 1-866-506-1949 or business@simonandschuster.com.

The Simon & Schuster Speakers Bureau can bring authors to your live event. For more information or to book an event contact the Simon & Schuster Speakers Bureau at 1-866-248-3049 or visit our website at www.simonspeakers.com.

Interior design by Jaime Putorti

Manufactured in the United States of America

10 9 8 7 6 5 4 3 2 1

Library of Congress Cataloging-in-Publication Data
Bell, Taylor.
  Dirty rush : a novel / Taylor Bell. -- First Gallery Books trade paperback edition.
    pages cm
  ISBN 978-1-4767-7528-9 (paperback) -- ISBN 978-1-4767-7571-5 (ebook)
  I. Title.
PS3602.E4553D57 2015
813'.6--dc23
                                              2014027605

ISBN 978-1-4767-7528-9
ISBN 978-1-4767-7571-5(ebook)

Dedicated to Miley Cyrus

Contents

FOREWORD BY REBECCA MARTINSON   xiii

1. TEQUILA, LIME JUICE, AND ADDERALL   1

2. TONIGHT'S CHOICES, TOMORROW'S FACEBOOK POSTS   17

3. HIIIIIIIIIIIIIIIIIIIIIIIIIIIIII . . .   28

4. I'M JUST ADVOCATING FOR LESS DRAKE AND MORE TUPAC   39

5. "SICK" AS IN "FUN"   48

6. POSSIBLY ONE OF THE BEST NIGHTS OF MY LIFE   66

7. COLLEGE GIRLS ARE CONSTANTLY
COMPLAINING ABOUT . . . EVERYTHING   74

8. SARAH   87

9. KIND OF ADULTS   93

10. SHARKS IN J.CREW   102

11. HAVE FUN YOU GUYS!!   116

12. COMPLETE SILENCE AND TOTAL DARKNESS   126

13. Y'ALL, ARE WE FIGHTING?   134

14. SISTERLY LOVE   140

15. PROMISES   148

16. FROZEN-YOGURT MACHINES   155

17. SHE'S LIKE SMART-STUPID   165

18. THE BZ GIRL   181

19. VIRAL   190

20. NORMAL HUMAN BEINGS DO CRAZY SHIT SOMETIMES   203

21. UNICORNS, FETTUCCINE ALFREDO, AND A COFFIN   212

22. GUILTY   224

23. IT'S GOING TO BE SUPER AWKWARD   230

24. LET'S DO THIS, BITCHES   240

ACKNOWLEDGMENTS   251

From: Martinson, Rebecca
Sent: Thursday, April 18, 2013 10:30 AM
To: Undisclosed Recipients
Subject: We fucking suck so far

If you just opened this like I told you to, tie yourself down to whatever chair you're sitting in, because this email is going to be a rough fucking ride.

We have been FUCKING UP in terms of nighttime events and general social interactions with Sigma Nu. I've been getting texts on texts about people LITERALLY being so fucking AWKWARD and so fucking BORING. If you're reading this right now and saying to yourself "But oh em gee, Becca, I've been having so much fun with my sisters this week!," then punch yourself in the face right now so that I don't have to fucking find you on campus to do it myself.

This week is about fostering relationships in the Greek community, and that's not fucking possible if you're going to stand around and talk to each other and not our matchup. Newsflash you stupid cocks: FRATS DON'T

LIKE BORING SORORITIES. Oh wait, DOUBLE FUCKING NEWSFLASH: SIGMA NU IS NOT GOING TO WANT TO HANG OUT WITH US IF WE FUCKING SUCK, which by the way in case you're an idiot and need it spelled out for you, WE FUCKING SUCK SO FAR.

This also applies to you little shits that have talked openly about post-gaming at a different frat IN FRONT OF SIGMA NU BROTHERS. Are you people fucking retarded? That's not a rhetorical question, I LITERALLY want you to email me back telling me if you're mentally slow so I can make sure you don't go to any more nighttime events. If Sigma Nu openly said "Yeah we're gonna invite Zeta over," would you be happy? WOULD YOU? No you wouldn't, so WHY THE FUCK WOULD YOU DO IT TO THEM?? IN FRONT OF THEM?!! First of all, you SHOULDN'T be post-gaming at other frats, I don't give a FUCK if your boyfriend is in it, if your brother is in it, or if your entire family is in that frat. YOU DON'T GO. YOU. DON'T. GO. And you ESPECIALLY do fucking NOT convince other girls to leave with you.

"But Rebecca!," you say in a whiny little bitch voice to your computer screen as you read this email, "I've been cheering on our teams at all the sports, doesn't that count for something?" NO YOU STUPID FUCKING ASS HATS, IT FUCKING DOESN'T. DO YOU WANNA KNOW FUCKING WHY?!! IT DOESN'T COUNT BECAUSE YOU'VE BEEN FUCKING UP AT SOBER FUCKING

EVENTS TOO. I've not only gotten texts about people being fucking WEIRD at sports (for example, being stupid shits and saying stuff like "durr, what's kickball?" is not fucking funny), but I've gotten texts about people actually cheering for the opposing team. The opposing. Fucking. Team. ARE YOU FUCKING STUPID?!! I will fucking cunt punt the next person I hear about doing something like that.

"Ohhh, I'm now crying because your email has made me oh so so sad." Well good. If this email applies to you in any way, meaning if you are a little asswipe that stands in the corners at night or if you're a weird shit that does weird shit during the day, this following message is for you:

DO NOT GO TO TONIGHT'S EVENT.

I'm not fucking kidding. Don't go. Seriously, if you have done ANYTHING I've mentioned in this email and have some rare disease where you're unable to NOT do these things, then you are HORRIBLE, I repeat, HORRIBLE PR FOR THIS CHAPTER. If you are one of the people that have told me "Oh nooo boo hoo I can't talk to boys I'm too sober," then I pity you because I don't know how you got this far in life, and with that in mind don't fucking show up unless you're going to stop being a goddamn cock block for our chapter. Seriously. I swear to fucking God if I see anyone being a goddamn boner at tonight's event, I will tell you to leave even if you're sober. I'm not even kidding. Try me.

And for those of you who are offended at this email, I would apologize but I really don't give a fuck. Go fuck yourself.

—Martinson

Foreword

BY REBECCA MARTINSON

In the event that you're either fucking stupid or blind and deaf, my name is Rebecca Martinson and I wrote that fine piece of Shakespeare-quality literature to my ex-sorority sisters awhile back. You know the email—the one Academy Award–nominated actor Michael Shannon read while channeling his inner serial killer on Funny or Die. Yeah, not gonna lie, he got it spot-on. I was dead fucking serious when I sent that email to my entire sorority LISTSERV, to the point where I was ready to go invest in a brand-spankin'-new pair of steel-toed boots in case any cunts needed a good punt.

I remember spending the rest of that day giving exactly zero fucks about every text and every email that I got, because 90 percent of them were along the lines of "Errmagherd, Rebecca, people are upset! They're crying! The fucking apocalypse is coming because of your email!" Well, good! People should've been crying. I mean, for fuck's sake, I warned them in advance to buckle their seat belts; it's not my problem if they can't follow directions, now is it?

In all seriousness, though, I was genuinely pissed. I cared so much about that sorority that to see people acting like turds with Asperger's syndrome just set me off, and clearly I'm not a pretty picture when I'm mad. Girls shunned me, looked the other way when I walked by, the whole shebang. But I didn't care. I said what needed to be said. If people chose to make me a social pariah because of it, then more power to them—go have fun scissoring in the chapter-house closets instead of talking to boys.

And then the shitstorm hit: my face on the news, plastered all over the Internet, fricking Jon Stewart saying "cunt punt" on *The Daily Show*. I had people ambushing me left and right trying to get me on their television show for an interview, wanting pictures with "The Deranged Sorority Girl," hitting me up to make me the star of my own reality TV show . . . But mostly the only thing I wanted to do was sleep. Believe it or not, it's exhausting to have the majority of the country screaming at you, albeit out of earshot. I didn't care about the fame—or, rather, infamy. I didn't care about appearing on television. Was getting a call from the producers at *Jimmy Kimmel* cool? Fuck yeah. But all I cared about right then was how shitty I'd unintentionally made my chapter look.

Which brings us to this fine piece of literature . . . When I was asked to write the Foreword for Taylor Bell's book, I was skeptical. No one ever gets sorority life right when it comes to putting it down in words, everything always turns into drunk chicks making out at parties while wearing Greek letters. So I said I'd be happy to write a Foreword . . . but only if the book was actually an accurate depiction of sorority life.

And you know what? This book fucking tells it like it fucking is. You won't find anything in here about how all sorority girls are vacuously stupid. You won't find anything in here about midnight pillow fights between girls dressed solely in their bras and panties. And you sure as fuck won't read anything about how a sorority girl's sole purpose in life is to be perpetually drunk and do the spread eagle for wasted frat bros. What you will find, however, is a story that shows the bonds that form over time between sorority women, and how making the simple decision to join Greek life can change a person in more positive ways than I could have ever imagined. Even though I was only in a sorority for a year, I have to admit that I left a better person than I was when I joined.

I'll leave you with this simple quote. It's something all sorority women have heard, but I don't think anyone ever gives any thought to how true it is.

"From the outside looking in, you can never understand it. From the inside looking out, you can never explain it."

If you weren't in a sorority, this book is your only chance at understanding Greek life. And if you were, you'll be blown away by how much of this makes total fucking sense.

Okay. I'm done. You can start reading, ya fuckin' assclown.

Dirty Rush

1.

TEQUILA, LIME JUICE, AND ADDERALL

"Name?" he asked.

"Taylor Bell."

He pretended to squint down at his clipboard, using it as an excuse to give me an up-down scan. Mirrored Ray-Bans sat low on his nose and LEGALIZE COCAINE was printed in bold black letters on his neon green tank top.

"Hmmm . . . Taco Bell," he said, smirking and still eyeing me, "I don't see any Taco Bells on the list, but you have an honest face and an honest . . . ass, so I'm gonna go ahead and let you in."

"I'm honored, thanks." He opened the door to the house, and I could immediately feel the mayhem booming inside. There was no turning back. I was going to a frat party, the end. I took a deep breath and stepped into the madness.

The house was a massive Victorian mansion with a vaulted foyer that featured one of those huge curved staircases that you only see in movies. There were two hallways, which must've led to the first-floor bedrooms, branching out from either side of the main room. It wasn't hard to imagine a century's worth of kids getting hammered in here, hiding behind the illusion of public service. The general scent of the house, however, was equal parts locker room and Victoria's Secret, and my sandals were sticking to the booze-soaked floor (#gross). My plan was to smile at all the drunk people, stay for ten minutes or until I found Jack, and get the fuck out.

I smoothed my dress and gauged the vibe of the party— it was a raucous symphony of electronic music and the wild screams of college kids in the prime of their lives. Decorations were sparse except for fog machines in every corner and one enormous disco ball. A DJ booth had been set up, and some Skrillex song was blasting from enormous speakers that hung from the ceiling. There were girls everywhere. Dancing on tables, grinding on guys, and taking selfies. Two of them were making out with each other while taking selfies.

"Boom! Those are some gold-medal gazongas!" an overweight, overly confident bro slurred in my direction. He was flanked by two other kind-of-fat guys who raised their Solo cups in my direction as if to congratulate me.

"Thank you?" I said, offering up a half smile. Even though he was clearly drunk, it seemed polite to accept his compliment.

Obviously the party was not designed with sobriety in mind,

so I went looking for a drink. Luckily, lining the walls of the main room were a bunch of lanky boys with mediocre faces holding silver trays with Solo cups filled to the brim with a suspect red liquid. They looked like twelve-year-olds. A shirtless, kind-of cute blond dude with big teeth leaned in toward me and grinned.

"'Sup, hot stuff? Drink?"

"Sure. Thanks," I said, grabbing a Solo cup off the tray. I took a sip. It tasted like rubbing alcohol, sugar, and sadness. Downing one would've been blackout city, so I put the cup back on his tray. "Just kidding. What else you got?"

"Keg's in the back," he said, motioning with the tray. A few cups toppled over, sloshing red punch down his arm. "Shit!"

"HEYYYY, RUSSELL SPROUT!" a familiar voice shouted. "What'd I tell you about spilling?" Suddenly, Jack Swanson, the reason I'd come to this godforsaken party to begin with, appeared in front of me, even more handsome than I'd remembered. I'd only met Jack two days earlier, when he sat next to me in my women's studies class, but I'd spent almost every hour since then wondering if he'd invited me to this party because he liked me or because it was his job as a frat boy to get wide-eyed freshman girls to the house. I was never the type to obsess over guys, but I was going with it. Jack had the type of smile that stuck in your brain for days on end.

He slung his big arm around Russell, who was shitfaced. Cute, but shitfaced, and he suddenly looked almost scared.

"Sir! Um . . . uhh . . . don't spill?" offered Russell.

"Correct. Now, please apologize to my friend Taylor here."

"Sorry, Taylor."

"Also, Sprout, do you mind doing one more little favor?"

"Yes, sir."

"So, you do mind?"

"No, sir. I meant no, sir, I don't mind."

"Great. Drop and give me fifty."

Without even a moment's hesitation, Russell turned, handed his tray to the pledge next to him, dropped to the floor, and started doing push-ups.

"I'm gonna need to hear you count," Jack said, crossing his arms and taking a step back to survey the push-ups. Russell looked like he was having a hard time. His face was turning red and he was panting.

"Five . . . six . . . seven . . . eight . . ."

"That's better. Hey, Taylor." Jack smiled, turned toward me, and placed a foot on Russell's back, crossing his arms. "Glad you could make it to our little get-together. I thought you weren't into the 'frat scene,' " he said, making air quotes.

"I'm not, but I thought I'd try something new."

"Well, I'm glad to see you have an adventurous spirit."

"Adventure's my middle name." I smiled back at him, immediately regretting my words.

He laughed a bit. "Alright. Noted."

Jack was so not my type, but there was something about him that gave me serious butterflies. He was dreamy, and I never say guys are dreamy. His skin was golden, maybe from being on a boat all summer, and his eyes were blue and kind. Even though Jack was acting like a typical bro, I could tell there was something else there. It was actually kind of confusing.

"Where's your drink?" he asked.

"Well, I did have the pleasure of sampling the rape juice, if that's what you mean. It was delicious but a bit too sweet for my taste. I'm gonna grab a beer. You want one?"

"No, no, no, that's not how this works. I retrieve the beers; you drink them. Not the other way around."

"Well, then, yes, please."

"Dope. Be right back."

And with that, Jack took his foot off of Russell's back and disappeared into the mass of bodies.

Russell made a loud guttural sound mid-push-up and a fountain of pink vomit shot out of his mouth onto the floor in front of me. I jumped back, barely dodging the spray of puke headed toward my sandals. As much as I wanted to wait for Jack, the toxic odor rising from Russell's mess encouraged a change in locale. Standing next to a puker is not a good look for anyone. I slowly backed away, mumbling, "Feel better."

"HEY, FRESHMAN!" I heard a voice scream. I turned around to see a kind-of-pretty, kind-of-short brunette making a beeline for me with a smile on her face. She was sporting a short J.Crew skirt and a polo. She hugged me and laughed. "I'm Meg. How autistic is this party?"

"It's definitely on the spectrum."

"What?"

"Um . . . nothing. Sorry, have we met?" I asked her as she pulled me into a corner.

"Nope, but it's your lucky day. I'm gonna be your Big Sis. Or at least I'll probably be your Big. Or at least I reallllly think I should be your Big because you're fucking cute as fuck." She grabbed me by the elbow and started weaving us through the crowd, hopefully toward the kitchen, because I still needed a drink. "Please tell me you didn't drink the jungle juice."

"Um, no, but you must be mistaking me for someone else. I haven't rushed or gotten a bid to pledge or whatever. I don't really—"

"Oh, it's okay. No one has yet."

"Rushed?"

"Yesssss," Meg whispered.

"Oh."

"But you def will. Rush Beta Zeta, that is. Aaaaaand we're totally not talking about this now because we don't want to be involved in a dirty rush scandal. Dealing with the Panhel is never cute. Trust," she said as she pulled out her phone and quickly responded to a text message. "Excuse me!" she yelled at a guy and girl attempting to dance while eating each other's faces on the dance floor. The girl looked up at us, squealed, and went in for a drunken hug.

"Meg!"

"Sabrina! Please stop dry humping Benjamin on the dance floor. It's gross. You need to set a good example. There are children present," she nodded in my direction.

The girl looked at us sheepishly.

"I kid! I kid!" Meg roared with laughter. Then, without missing a beat, she put her free hand on the girl's shoulder, got up in her face, and calmly said, "Please use a condom tonight, love." As we walked away, she turned to me, "That's Sabrina. She's a junior BZ and has been with her boyfriend, Ben, since high school. They fuck anywhere and everywhere and have had, like, ten pregnancy scares. So retarded."

"Cool?"

"Yeah!" Meg said enthusiastically. I had no idea how to respond to this.

"So what's this about me rushing?" I asked instead.

"Wait, you're Taylor Bell, right? The girl with, like, a three-generation legacy?"

"I guess that's one way to describe me."

"Your sisters, Kelly and Jess, are fucking Beta Zeta legends. I never met Jess, but Kelly had the best tit-to-waist ratio I've ever seen. Yours isn't bad either."

I looked down at my white dress and back up at Meg. "Thank you?"

I was a little weirded out by Meg's knowledge of my family's history, but she was totally right. I was the fifth woman in my family to attend Central Delaware University. My grandmother, mom, and two sisters had all graduated from CDU and were all proud members of the Beta Zeta sorority. I was a legacy, I guess, but my decision to come to this school had nothing to do with a sorority. I'd been accepted to a bunch of great colleges besides CDU, but this was the only one that offered me a full academic scholarship, and the idea of having zero student loans to pay off when I graduated was just too good to pass up. So, ironically, here I was, following in the collegiate footsteps of basically all the women in my entire family. At a fucking frat party.

Meg pushed our way through a line in the kitchen and started pumping a keg. "So you're definitely rushing. You'd be retarded not to. God, I'm sorry for saying 'retarded' so much. I know I'm not supposed to say that word. I mean, for all I know you have a very retarded cousin or something. But, like, it's the most accurate way to describe something that's actually retarded, you know? Like this party. And the thought of you not rushing a sorority you can clearly get into and pull serious rank."

"Rank?"

"Yes, retard. Rank." Meg handed me a beer.

"What do you mean?" I asked, genuinely intrigued.

"Look, you obvi didn't hear this from me, but if you rush Beta Zeta, not only will you get a bid in, like, five seconds, but you'll basically be able to do and say whatever you want. Colette will have no choice but to be nice to you, which is not easy for her. And besides, you're super fucking cute and you look smart but not in an annoying way."

"Thanks," I replied. "And Colette is who, exactly?"

"Oh, Colette Winter's basically the unofficial boss bitch of the Beta Zeta chapter here at CDU. She doesn't hold a title, but everyone listens to her anyway. She can be a cunty fucking whore sometimes, but I get it. That's how it works in sororities—you'll see. Presidents do paperwork and go to meetings, Colette gets shit done and makes girls cry in public."

"Heavy is the head that wears the crown," I said half-kidding.

Meg looked at me as if I'd just said something to her in Mandarin, before responding with a loud, "Exactly!"

I took a sip of my beer and looked around the party. There was a boy drunkenly trying to break-dance on the kitchen floor, alone. He was shirtless but appeared to be wearing some sort of boobie-tassels over his nipples.

"No offense, but all of this isn't really for me. I think it's sweet that you guys would want me to join, but I'm not my grandma or my mom or my sisters. I'm not really sure that, um, Greek life is my scene."

"Then what is your scene? Because at present, it's a frat party."

"The truth is, I kind of just came here to see a guy, who I think I'm gonna go try and find now. Thanks for the beer, though."

I had walked away from Meg and back into the throngs of bodies dancing when I started to notice just how sweaty everyone at this party was. I'm not a big fan of sweat, sweaty strangers, or plumes of pot smoke blown into my face, so I decided to remove myself from the dance floor pronto and check out the rest of the house and maybe (hopefully) run into Jack again. I spotted a tight, dark hallway that seemed to lead to a rear living room, and headed in that direction, pulling my bag closer to me because it was so packed in there. My phone was buzzing. I managed to pull it out and saw that I had three texts from Jonah, my best friend from high school who was also now a freshman at CDU. We didn't exactly plan on following identical academic trajectories, but we'd done almost everything together in high school, so it made sense. Most of our friends from home thought that we'd end up getting married, but most of our friends also still thought Jonah was straight.

Jonah 10:15PM Where r u? I'm bored.

Jonah 10:16PM My roommate keeps farting in our room and not saying anything. So awk

Jonah 10: 29PM where are u??????

Shit. Fuck. Shit. I'd totally flaked on Jonah. We were supposed to hang out, and then I decided to take up a virtually
random frat guy on his invite instead.

Taylor 10:30PM Are u sitting down?

Jonah 10:31PM Yes

Taylor 10:31PM I'm at a frat party. U wanna come?

Jonah 10:32PM Are you ok? Is this a joke? What happened to getting wasted and watching Rosemary's Baby?

Taylor 10:34PM I ♥ you. But this is just as fun and scary as Rosemary's. So just come.

Jonah 10:37PM I hate you. Where is it?

Taylor 10:37PM Omega Sig

Jonah 10:38PM As if I know where that is

Jonah 10:38PM Address?

I sent him a pin of where I was, shoved my phone back into
my bag, and continued to push through the packed hallway. My
plan to snoop around was thwarted when I walked into the living room and realized I was going to have to somehow avoid
getting roped into playing Twister with a group of bikini-clad,
slutty-looking freshman girls and some fraternity dudes. I had
no idea people still played Twister. One of the frat guys waved
at me to join in. Fortunately, a girl's tit fell out of her top as she
was reaching for a green dot, which distracted him, allowing me
to snake back out of the living room past a group of kids bong-
ing beers. I wondered whether the girls had brought their own

bikinis or if the frat had provided them. On closer inspection, I noticed that the bikini bottoms were stamped with OMEGA SIGMA across the ass. Wow. That answered that question.

I walked into a quiet, dimly lit hallway that was surprisingly not crowded. Then, out of nowhere, I heard something very loud and very fast coming toward me. I quickly threw myself backward against the wall and hoped for the best. A beat-up shopping cart crammed with dudes came flying past me, stopped short, and launched its passengers into an inflatable kiddie pool filled with Jell-O in the kitchen. A crowd surrounding the pool exploded in excitement.

Was this a real party, or a movie about a frat party? I couldn't tell the difference anymore. It also occurred to me that wearing a white dress had been a huge mistake. When my eyes adjusted to the darkness, I spotted an exit sign at the end of the hallway and started running toward it, hoping for a good, clean escape. But as the door swung open and I stepped out of the house I saw Meg and a hot, model-y–looking guy standing right in front of me, making out. Meg noticed me and freaked.

"Taylor! Do not tell me you're actually trying to leave."

"Ummmmm . . ."

"You're not even tipsy!"

"Okay."

Meg pulled a small flask out of her Michael Kors Monogram clutch, took a shot from it, and offered it up to me.

"What is this?" I asked.

"Tequila, lime juice, and homemade Adderall solution. It's my secret recipe. Go ahead, you'll like it."

"Text me," said the model-y guy.

"Shut up, Mark. Can't you see I'm fucking busy?" said Meg.
I took a small sip. It wasn't horrible.

"See? Now come the fuck on, you didn't think this was the actual party, did you?"

I guess I wasn't going home quite yet . . .

After walking back into the house and weaving through a labyrinth of hallways and strange, packed bedrooms, Meg and I arrived at a closed green door.

"You ready?" she asked slyly, taking another swig from her flask and handing it back to me. I took another, slightly bigger, sip.

"Not really."

She pushed the door open and we walked down a long spiral staircase with cold stone walls on either side. As we descended, I heard girls laughing and the thumping bass of that Kendrick Lamar song every white person I know is obsessed with. We walked into a room full of scantily clad bodies. Some of them were dancing, some of them were sitting at tables playing cards and drinking. This crowd was much more attractive than the rest of the party upstairs. It was like I'd been upgraded from coach to first class.

"Meg!!" two identical girls screamed in unison. They were both in jeans and tank tops and they were coming right for us.

"Ladies! You look amazing!" Meg screamed back at them. The music was insanely loud. "This is Taylor Bell, Kelly's sister. Third-generation legacy, and honestly, how fucking cute is she?!"

"Love it!" said one of the twins. I hadn't realized it until I was standing next to them, but they were both so tall.

"I'm Stephanie and this is Olivia, we're twins. Obviously," said the other as they both laughed. I went in for a handshake, but both of them just looked at me, confused. It was weird.

"So, Asher texted me two hours ago and said he was probably coming," Stephanie said, smiling. "Then I texted him back 'Can't wait to see you' with a smiley face, and now he just has his little thought bubble there. It's been like that for at least an hour. Is this, like, a power move? Should I just kill myself?" She made a pouty face.

For some reason, her question made me laugh really hard, which made them all start laughing. Their closeness was kind of charming.

"As you can see, Steph is an actual insane person," Olivia said, putting her arm around her sister. "Have fun tonight and ask us any questions you want. We're good girls, we promise!"

"Nice meeting you guys," I said to the twins as they turned and danced their way across the room.

"Okay," Meg said, grabbing me again by the elbow and walking me through the room. "Those are our twins. They come as a package. Steph's not a slut but she loves to fuck, so that would explain this Asher person she mentioned—always a new guy with her—very liberated when it comes to the sex. Olivia is the brains of the operation. She's literally a genius. She had the idea for Facebook before Facebook was even invented. She was six. I'm not even joking."

"Wow, that's amazing—"

"And that over there is Colette. You want her to think you're pretty and you want to be friends with her. She was basically your sister's bestie last year. They co-chaired our biggest annual event with the children's hospital. It was amazing. Babe Walker did the keynote speech, Diplo deejayed, and a lot of cancer kids lived because of them. I'm sure she'll love you."

We slowly walked toward a very tall, very thin girl who had her back to us. She was wearing a cropped sweater with a short skirt and suede ankle boots and had the shiniest hair I'd ever seen, tied up in a tight ponytail. She must've sensed our presence, because as we got a little closer she turned around to face us.

"You must be Kelly's skinnier, prettier sister," Colette said, staring right at me. "Just kidding." She smiled.

It hit me immediately that I'd seen this girl once in the Beta Zeta house when I was visiting Kelly. She was unforgettable.

"Um . . ." I was speechless. Colette was one of those girls who knew that she was gorgeous and loved it. I was in awe. Her Chloé perfume was intoxicating.

Luckily Meg chimed in, "Yup, this is Taylor, Kelly's little sister. The new face of Beta Zeta."

"Is that so?" Colette raised an eyebrow. This girl had obviously spent hours in front of the mirror perfecting her bitch face.

"Well, I don't know if I'm going to rush yet. I'm still figuring it out."

"Don't be an idiot. This school is boring as fuck if you're not Greek," said Colette.

"Totally," added a very excited Meg. "Beta Zeta is the main reason I came to this school. We're good girls, and honestly, once you're a sister, you're kinda set for life. But you already know that, Taylor. You're a purebred, babe!" She turned to Colette, who was making eyes with a linebacker-looking guy across the room.

"How *is* your sister, by the way?" Colette asked, seeming very uninterested.

"She's great. Still in Zambia, interning away."

"Oh . . . right." Colette seemed confused. "That's great," she continued, "good for her."

"Yeah. I'm really impressed by the work they're doing out there," I offered.

"Well, this all sounds amazing, but would you guys excuse me for just a second?" Colette asked as she gave us each a limp hug before walking over to the baby-faced bodybuilder in a trucker hat. Someone tapped on my shoulder.

"Looks like you made it into the cool kids' club."

It was Jack, looking a little more disheveled but no less hot.

"Is that what this is?" I was so happy that he'd found me, but did my best to hide it.

"I walked around with your beer for about ten minutes looking for you, but I see you've already been adopted by the one and only Meg Landry. What's up, Meg?" he said, pulling Meg in for a bear hug and kissing her on the cheek.

"Jack and I bonded freshman year over a joint appreciation for Fleetwood Mac and Miller High Life, didn't we, Jacko?" Meg said, taking a sip of a vodka rocks that she'd managed to grab somewhere.

"That is technically a true statement," Jack said, looking at me. "Although I don't like to publicize the fact that I wanna bone Stevie Nicks. So, thanks for that, Megs."

God. He was beyond cute. His smile was so disarming and genuine. I couldn't help but imagine what it would be like to lay around in bed with Jack all day, drink some beers, and let "Landslide" play on repeat.

"Jack!!!" The sound of a shrieking voice coming from behind me snapped me out of my daydream. I felt two hands shove me from behind. Hard.

I lost my footing and went flying past Jack and Meg, crashed through several full drinks that spilled all over me, and then snagged my foot on some wires that were apparently connected to the speakers, abruptly cutting the music and silencing the room as I careened face-first into two nasty old couch cushions. I saw darkness and smelled a nauseating mixture of sweat, mildew, and farts. I didn't lift my head, but I could feel that everyone in that basement was looking at me.

FML.

2.

TONIGHT'S CHOICES, TOMORROW'S FACEBOOK POSTS

Get up, Taylor, I thought to myself. Stand up and tell everyone that you're okay and immediately get the fuck out of here, then move to a different continent.

"Shit," I said as I lifted my head from the couch, directly into view of a girl straddling a guy's crotch. Oh God. I'd landed directly next to Sabrina, the girl from upstairs who'd had all the abortion scares, and her boyfriend.

"Are you okay?" Sabrina asked, dismounting her boyfriend and pulling down her skirt.

"I . . . I'm fine," I lied. I'd never been less fine. I stood up and dusted myself off, taking in the fact that the entire party had come to a halt. Almost everyone in the room was staring at me and snickering. I scanned the room for Jack. He was in a corner talking to some girl I didn't recognize. It was immediately and unavoidably clear from their body language that they had definitely seen each other naked. Wait. What the fuck was going on? Why had he flirted with me in class and invited me to his house if he was already with somebody? Would he really be into a drunk girl in a denim miniskirt and plastic flip-flops? I was fuming and embarrassed, but I had to hide it. Really, I just wanted to die.

Allow me to introduce myself: Taylor Bell, the naive college freshman who just made a total ass of herself at her first frat party.

My dress was totally ruined, covered in brown stains and reddish liquid. Both of my knees were scraped and bloody, my whole body was pounding. A waterfall of tears was trying to push its way out from behind my eyeballs. How was I going to walk through the party and back to my dorm in this state? I would never be able to live this down. And all because I wanted to get closer to Jack.

"Okay! We're clearly over this!" I heard a voice say, as Meg steered me away from the couch and toward the back of the room. Unfortunately, that meant we had to walk past Jack and Random Girl. He looked at me with a pout and mouthed *Are you okay?* before walking away with the girl.

I was not okay.

Meg speedily led me to the quietest corner of the room.

"Babe. Are you okayyyyy?" Meg sang/pleaded, looking me up and down.

"Yeah. I'm fine."

"But . . . you're bleeding."

"I know that!" I snapped. Then, off her shocked expression, "I'm sorry, I should really go. Is there a side entrance or a back door I can sneak out of? I really don't want to walk through that party looking like—"

"Noooooo. No, no, no, no. Absolutely not."

"No, I should really go," I told her. "Thanks for everything. Tonight was actually fun, until whatever that was . . . happened. Have a good time."

"Are you sure? The night's just getting started," Meg pled.

"Yeah, I'm fine. I just . . . I don't know."

"What? You can tell me."

"It's nothing, I just . . . I came here tonight because Jack invited me. We have a class together. I thought he liked me and now I feel like a total idiot."

"Jack? Oh, babe. No, no, no. I will not have you sitting in bed with bloody knees, watching Netflix, and crying about a boy on a Thursday night. No. That's not an option." Meg put her drink up to my mouth, forcing a big gulp.

"I don't even know who pushed me," I said.

"I hate to say this," Meg said, putting her hand in mine, "but it's that girl Jack's talking to right now. I think they went to high school together or something."

This night kept finding ways to get worse.

But then, like magic, Steph and Olivia popped out of the crowd on either side of me, followed shortly by Colette in all her hair's glimmering glory.

"We just saw what happened and you definitely shouldn't leave yet," Olivia chirped.

She put a limp hand on my shoulder. "Don't even worry about it. Jack's a flirt and can be an ass and that skank's a Beta Pi and she's really stupid, like actually dumb. You should see her Instagram. It's all pictures of Ke$ha and inspirational quotes and cats that aren't even hers."

The "skank" must've heard Olivia's Instagram insult, because she approached us with a scowl on her face to end all scowls.

"What'd you say, bitch?" she spat at Olivia, pushing her from behind. I guess this girl was really into pushing. Is this about to be a fight? Is this what these girls do? I was scared.

"Hello, Blair. Belligerent as per usual, I can see," said a very serious Colette, positioning herself directly in front of her.

"Don't start with me, Colette, this is not about you," Blair said, trying to push past Colette, who was firmly standing her ground.

"That's what you don't seem to understand. In fact, this seems to be a recurring issue with you, Blair. I don't think you're able to grasp the concept that when you fuck with one of us, you fuck with all of us. Unfortunately, that means you have to deal with me."

"Who even *is* that girl and why are you acting like her mom? Can you just get out of my fucking way?" attempted a flustered Blair.

"Not until I let you know that from here on out, there will be no trace of you at this house or anywhere near a Beta Zeta sister without major repercussions."

Meg put her hand on my shoulder and whispered, "Watch the master at work."

"Because," Colette continued, "if you do make the grave and hazardous decision to involve yourself in any of my sisters' lives,

I will personally organize and ensure your social ostracism. The truth is, Blair Witch Project, you're bad business for all of us. I'm surprised you haven't been expelled yet for last semester's string of D's in not one, not two, but all five of your 101 courses."

"Oh, so you're stalking me now?"

"Honestly, it's quite an accomplishment to be that lazy. It's also quite an accomplishment to give an entire varsity crew team chlamydia. So, congrats."

"Yeah, thanks a lot for that!" screamed someone from the crowd.

"You short bitch!" screamed another random voice.

Blair was utterly speechless and turning ghost white. But it wasn't over.

"I can't have you coming to another event and causing these scenes. Lest we forget the Kappa Date Party last spring when you ended up in the back of a cop car for shitting in public."

"That's not even true."

"I'm not saying it's true. I'm saying it might be true, which is actually worse."

Everyone in the room was now watching the drama. The attention had shifted from my fall, thank the Lord. I scanned the room for Jack, but he was nowhere to be found.

"So, pretty please," Colette said with a big smile, "before you end up doing something else trashy and shameful, take your Abercrombie skirt and the advanced cultures of mold growing on those wretched Old Navy flip-flops, and get the fuck away from all of us. Preferably until the end of time."

All the color had drained from Blair's face; a single tear rolled down her cheek.

"You're a cunt," she whispered.

"Yes, I am. Now I think you should apologize to Taylor for pushing her and ruining her dress. And then you can apologize to everyone in here for being a sloppy whore in general."

Blair turned her low gaze toward me. "I'm sorry."

"What are you sorry for?" Colette nudged.

"I'm sorry for . . . for . . ."

"For generally being a sloppy . . ."

"A sloppy whore."

"And also?"

"And for pushing you and ripping your dress. It's a cute dress. Was."

"That wasn't so hard, was it? Now, do the right thing and leave."

Blair hung her head and walked out. Holy fuck.

"And that's how it's done," Meg said, turning to me and winking.

Colette pulled out her phone and started texting.

"What size are you? A two?" she asked.

"Um, yeah. I'm a two. Why?"

"We're taking care of this," Meg said excitedly. "We look out for each other. When a sister is in danger of embarrassment, humiliation, or excessive partying to the point of potential mouth-herpe contraction, one of us is always there to rescue her."

"Well, thanks. That was really embarrassing."

"We know," Colette said with a bored look on her face.

Meg produced some sort of clear cocktail from behind her, handed it to me, and then clicked her cup against mine.

"We shall steadfastly love each other."

"What?" I asked.

"It's the Beta Zeta motto. We're not all greasy sluts in sweatpants and UGGs. Some sororities are real sisterhoods."

"She's almost here," Colette said to Olivia and Steph.

"Who's almost here?" I asked.

"Just come with us," said Olivia as she and Stephanie took me by the arms and led me back up the stairs to the entrance of the secret basement. Right as we were about to get to the top, the door opened to reveal a pint-size red-haired girl standing with a robe in one hand and a garment bag in the other.

"Hi, girls! Hi, Taylor; I'm Hailey. Put this on."

"Thank you, Hailey. Now shut the fuck up," Steph said, grabbing the robe and thrusting it into my hands.

"What's going on?" I asked, slipping the robe over my shoulders.

"Just put it on. Hailey is on Slop Patrol this semester. She's on call at every party in case of an emergency like your recent mishap, after which it is her job to show up and silently whisk you away to an undisclosed location, where she will help you get your shit together so that you don't end up looking like Amanda Bynes in tomorrow's Facebook posts," said Olivia giving Hailey a pointed look. "Thanks, hon," said Olivia.

"Oh, you're totes welcome—"

"Shut the fuck up, Hailey! No talking, remember?"

I put the robe on, and Steph nudged me toward Hailey, who reached out and grabbed my hand. I pulled the hood of the robe over my head, and Hailey quickly led me upstairs to a bathroom at the end of a hallway.

"Okay," Hailey said, locking the door behind us and assessing the train wreck that was me. "Meg said via text that you scraped your knees, but holy shit, girl, it looks like you raped your knees. Sit down."

I sat on the edge of the toilet. Hailey pulled a first-aid kit out of her backpack, knelt in front of me, poured some hydrogen peroxide onto a cotton pad, and started cleaning up my wounds.

"So are you rushing or what?" Hailey asked.

"I don't know . . . I hadn't planned on it." But I did know. I was not rushing.

"You're Taylor Bell, right? The girl who has, like, a huge legacy?"

"Yeah. Would you mind telling me how everyone knows that?"

"Everyone knows everything about everyone here." She threw the bloody wad of cotton into an overflowing trash can. "You're a fucking retard if you don't rush. It would be like Kate Middleton telling Prince William that she didn't want to marry him and, like, become the most powerful woman on earth."

"But she's not the most powerful woman on earth . . ." I said.

"But she is, if you think about it, you know?" She started dabbing Neosporin on the scrapes. "Like, if you were anyone else, you would have had to walk of shame yourself through that party, never to be seen or heard from again, and your only shot at Greek life would be joining an Asian sorority. Which is actually not an easy thing to do. They test your coding skills before you can even pledge. At least that's what I've heard." Hailey put Band-Aids on my knees and wrapped them both in gauze.

"So, I'm confused. Are you in Beta Zeta?"

"I rushed last year and didn't get Beta, so I'm kind of kissing ass this year. Basically, I'm the girls' Fairy Slop Mother. I see it as an internship. I mean, all I want to do tonight is get shitfaced and make out with this really hot Jewish kid from my econ class, but if I fuck up, Beta Zeta will shun me and everyone on campus will hate me and then I'll die all alone. Okay! Your knees are good to go. Sucks that you can't wear shorts or dresses for a month, 'cause you have cute legs."

Hailey unzipped the garment bag and pulled out a pair of high-waisted, flowy floral pants and a crop top and handed them to me. "This crop top will make your boobs look huge and fake, which is a good thing—trust."

Once I'd changed clothes, I realized Hailey was right. My boobs did look amazing. Normally I'd never wear something so Vanessa Hudgens-y, but I kind of loved the way I looked in this outfit. I felt like a different version of myself. I felt like a girl who could belong here.

There was a loud knock at the door.

Over the party's pumping music I heard someone shout: "It's us. Open the door, bitches!"

Hailey ran to the door and unlocked it. The door flew open to reveal Meg, flanked by Olivia and Steph.

"Oh my God, you look amazing!" Steph screamed.

My adrenaline had stopped pumping out of control and I could feel that my cheeks were their normal color again. These girls had just pulled me out of that type of awkward boy situation that can scar you for months. Maybe I didn't really know as much about Greek life as I thought—maybe these girls were actually good people, and maybe I'd been too quick to judge them.

As all these thoughts rushed through my head, Steph squeezed
my arm and leaned in to me.

"You wouldn't happen to have any coke, would you?"

"Not now, LiLo," Meg interjected. "We need to get her back
in the saddle."

When we got back down to the basement I could tell that the
makeover had worked. People's eyes were on me but it wasn't the
there's-the-girl-who-just-fell-on-her-face look, instead I was getting
jealous looks from the girls and wanna fuck looks from the guys. I
spotted Jack across the room. He was also looking at me. I averted
my eyes and put my hair up in a ponytail, trying to play it cool, but
I could see in my periphery that he was beelining toward me.

"Whoaaaaa," he said. "You clean up nice, huh?"

Ew, I thought. I hate when people say that.

"Thanks, Jack."

"So . . ."

"So . . ."

"So, like . . ."

"Are you having fun with your friend?" I asked.

"Oh, Blair? She's just a . . ."

"Friend?"

"Yeah. That's what I was going to say."

"Ah. Cute."

He may have been adorable, but Jack was not the conversa-
tionalist I'd met in class. He was drunk, however.

"You wanna come check out my room?"

"Hmmmmm. I think I'll pass."

I wanted to hang out with the Jack I thought I was meeting here, not the jackass he'd turned out to be.

"Tay!" Meg squealed, pushing her way toward us. "You have to come with me, there's an extremely babed-out business major who wants to meet you, and by 'meet you' I mean 'bone you.'"

As I was dragged away from Jack, I looked back just in time to hear him say, "See you in class, I guess?"

"Yeah." I flashed him a million-dollar smile. "I guess."

"Also," Meg said as we walked away from Jack, "did you invite someone named Jonah? The door guy just texted me. They're not letting him in."

3.

HIIIIIIIIIIIIIIIIIIIIIIIIIIIIIIIII . . .

"*C*an you please turn off your phone?"

Those are the words that woke me from the deepest sleep I'd ever been in.

"Taylor."

I did a quick body status check before opening my eyes.

"Taylor?"

Definitely hungover, definitely tired, my knees still felt like they'd been assaulted, but thankfully and perhaps most important, I recognized the feeling of my sheets against my skin. I was in my bed, in my dorm room. Thank you, Jesus, or whoever it was who got me home safe. The voice got louder.

"TAYLOR!"

I realized that the booming voice from across the room belonged to my generally quiet, adorably dweeby roommate, Morgan Hardy. She had short brown hair and a kind of smushed yet friendly face. She was not the type of girl who gave two fucks about how she presented and it totally worked for her. We didn't really know each other yet, but here she was screaming at me to wake up. Ugh, dorm life was a bizarre thing to get used to.

"What? I'm sleeping. Stop, seriously. Leave me alone."

"Your phone has been going off for, like, thirty minutes and it's really annoying. I'm trying to sleep."

Last night? Had that happened?

I couldn't tell if what I remembered was real or just an intense dream. It was this strange combination of nostalgia and feeling completely detached from the events that took place. Things could have taken a very dark turn for me, but Meg, Sabrina, Colette, and the twins made sure that didn't happen. The "incident" ended up being an afterthought—a minor blip, a footnote—to one of the craziest, most fun nights I'd had in a long time.

But holy shit, my head felt like it was in a fucking vise. Switching from beer to Meg's Adderall juice to vodka and sugar-free Red Bull to vodka and regular Red Bull to Jell-O shots had not been a good idea.

I needed to come out of my sheet cocoon, deal with the day, my hangover, and my annoyed roommate. It took a few moments to focus on any of my surroundings. Two plain wooden desks, two ugly beds, a mini fridge, and a weird framed poster of some ironic eighties movie called *The Lost Boys* hanging over Morgan's bed. I could really only muster enough energy to say one thing.

"I'm a cliché."

"Sorry to rain on your existential parade, but can you turn off your phone? Your choice of text alert leaves a lot to be desired." Morgan smiled.

"Yeah, sorry." I turned off the ringer.

The roommate situation could have been a lot worse. I lucked out. Jonah's roommate, Christopher, for example, had three gerbils that he slept with. So far, Morgan had actually been totally respectful, clean, logical, and fair in her cohabitational philosophy. She seemed sane and had already declared herself a poli-sci/ gender studies double major, and we hadn't even had our first full week of classes. Most mornings she was up and out by eight, so we didn't cross paths too much.

"I'm so hungover," I moaned.

"I'm so shocked."

"Sorry about my phone. I know we discussed being mindful of each other's sleeping schedules, but always feel free to just come over and turn off the ringer if that ever happens again."

"Oh great. Is this going to be happening a lot? Because it's a little bit hard to sleep when your roommate is sitting up in her bed at four in the morning eating a slice of pizza and watching *Pretty Little Liars* without headphones in."

"Oh my God. I did that?"

"Yeah, pretty much."

"Fuck me, I'm sorry. It's not really my style to go out that hard. I don't know what came over me."

"No worries. Have your fun. Freshman year, first frat party, I assume . . . Hot guys, pounding music, vomit. I get it. I tried to look for your phone while you were sleeping, but I think you

were on top of it and I didn't want to get fresh. We barely know
each other."

Another text popped up.

"I will definitely change that ringtone when I'm less hungover."

"Much appreciated."

It was from Jonah. His eighth.

Jonah 10:43AM Check Instagram

Jonah 10:48AM Did you check?

Jonah 10:48AM I tagged you in a few. Don't hate me.

Jonah 10:59AM Are you sleeping?

Jonah 11:31AM Tay?

Jonah 11:46AM I want Chuck Fils

Jonah 11:46AM *Chick-fil-A

Jonah 12:20PM I'm going to Chick-fil-A. Come

An hour later I was sitting across from Jonah, who, despite
having partied harder than I did last night, looked unscathed
by the debauchery. He was silly handsome and if he wasn't gay,
Jonah would've probably been the sluttiest jock at our high
school. Unfortunately, there hadn't been too many options for
him at Ballard.

We were both wearing the unofficial uniform of the American student. On him: his CDU Swimming sweatshirt and a pair
of Adidas track pants; on me: an oversized American Apparel

cardigan, a nice clean pair of Lululemon leggings, and I hate to admit this, but my favorite, four-year-old purple UGGs. My hair was still wet from my shower, up in a little bun. Before me was a deluxe chicken sandwich, a large waffle fries, and a large Dr Pepper. At that moment, as I took my first few bites, there wasn't a happier human being on earth. Chicken + Grease = Hangover Feeling Four Thousand Percent Better.

"God forgive us for momentarily succumbing to the institution of Chick-fil-A despite their appalling homophobic beliefs—" I said with my mouth full of food.

"Because this sandwich is so fucking good," Jonah interjected.

"Exactly," I said.

"Last night was insane," Jonah said as he began to devour his second spicy chicken biscuit.

"I know. But good insane. I was literally blackout and had to do some serious deleting and untagging on Facebook and Instagram on my walk over here."

"Me too. So, were all of those girls we were with last night BZs?"

I could sense a dig in Jonah's tone. He was never a big fan of Greek stuff—neither of us were.

"Yep. All of 'em."

"Did you know them from before? Through Kelly?"

"No. Literally, I met all of them last night for the first time. But they knew me."

"Is that the treatment they give to all legacies?"

"No idea. I mean, they all knew who I was because of Kelly, but still. It was for sure weird, but in a nice way."

"Very nice of them indeed. But also kinda twisted to see you all up in that sorority bullshit. You chilling with sorority girls was actually the most insane part of last night for me. More insane than that one dude's Jonas Brothers tattoo."

"How do you think I felt? It was like I was Cinderella and the rest of the girls were those tiny woodland creatures."

"Oh . . . I'm well aware. I saw the outfit they put you in. I felt like I was watching "Made: I Wanna Be in a Sorority" or some shit. It was mind-blowing. But you looked cute."

"Thanks, Jonie."

"You're not calling me Jonie anymore, remember?"

"But it's our thing, Jonie."

"Fine. Call me whatever you'd like, but just know that you're opening the floodgates of middle school nicknames."

"You wouldn't."

"Oh, I certainly would, Taylor the Flailer."

"That seizure was really scary!"

"Yeah, no shit, I was there. With the rest of Montgomery Middle. It was terrifying." Jonah flicked a half-eaten waffle fry at me.

"But at least you're starting to make a good impression here," he continued. "With your epic frat party basement fail, et cetera."

"You're totally right. First impressions are everything. So you must be feeling especially weird about how you had to have your best friend from high school get you in."

"Touché. That wasn't my shining moment."

"Let's pretend you didn't just say 'touché.' "

"I'm comfortable with that."

We both took long sips of our respective fountain sodas in an unspoken truce.

"So," I asked, "I know you're not really into the all-American thing, but meet anyone fun last night?"

"In a word . . . no," Jonah said confidently. "I'm not gonna meet a guy at a fucking frat party, that's for sure."

He went back to enjoying his calorie-castle. Jonah was on the swim team, so he could basically eat two of everything without ever gaining a pound. He was my oldest friend that I actually still liked. We'd both played in the jazz band at school, we were both huge Smashing Pumpkins fans, and we shared an obsession with *Breaking Bad* and *Real Housewives of Atlanta*. So naturally we spent a ton of time together.

"How were your classes this week?"

"Fine, I guess? I don't know."

"Which applied mathematics are you taking again?"

"Philosophy and Logic 116. It seems annoying so far."

"Any babes on the swim team?"

"Eh, there's one kid. He's Irish or something and definitely straight, but I'm not even gonna think about shitting where I eat."

"Fair. Are the other guys on the team cool?"

"Some are pretty cool, or funny or whatever. I'm still getting to know shit. It's actually all I've been focused on. I literally live in that pool." He sounded a bit defeated.

"Yeah, I've noticed."

"They told me I'd be able to have a life."

"So intense. I still don't really get sports."

"The coach has me slated for four events at our first meet.

I mean, it's only against other CDU students until the season officially starts, but still. It's tomorrow night, by the way. You should come."

"I'm there. Obviously."

"You wanna see a movie tonight? The new Wes Anderson looks pretty sweet . . ."

Right then, I heard someone knocking at the window near our table. I looked up and saw Stephanie and Olivia standing there looking at us. Steph was waving excitedly, while Olivia looked like she could give two shits. Steph hurried into the restaurant and up to our table; Olivia lit a cigarette.

"Hiiiiiiiiiiiiiiiiiiiiiiiiiiiiiiiii . . ." The word seemed to trail on forever as she scanned the restaurant, probably to check if she'd been spotted by anyone she knew. "You guys look super cute."

"Hey, Steph. What's up?"

"Sooooo good, thanks for asking! Olivia would've come in to say hi if it were any other restaurant."

"Oh, because they're anti-gay-marriage? I know, I'm embarrassed to be giving these people money myself, but I was so hungover—"

"Huh? No. It's because we aren't exactly supposed to be seen in fast-food places like this. It's like an unspoken rule."

"Wait. What?"

"Yeah, we aren't really supposed to go to places like this. It's, like . . . an unspoken rule," she repeated slowly.

"Wow. Really?"

"Yeah. You shouldn't be in here either. If you're planning on pledging."

"Are you serious?"

"Definitely serious. Colette is pretty strict about this stuff."

"Uh . . . okay. Thanks for the heads-up."

"Also, Meg texted this morning and said that we're fine with the Panhel or whatever about your situation."

"The Panhel?"

"Yup."

"I don't know what that is."

"You don't?"

"No. Am I supposed to?"

"The Panhellenic Association. All the national sororities fall under its jurisdiction. Basically, girls who are interested in Greek life technically have to go and 'visit' each sorority on campus before rushing. But since you're a major, major legacy and we love you so much, Meg said you don't have to go around and meet all the fucking tards at their weird special-ed houses."

"Wow. Cool . . . thanks for the update," I said as I sipped my Dr Pepper. Jonah was staring at Steph.

"We just wanted to make it easy on you. Plus, they owed us a favor in the Panhel office anyway."

"Thanks?"

"Fuck yeah thanks."

"Awesome. Well, thanks for stopping by and getting me all up to speed on everything."

"Oh my God, no problem. It was completely my pleasure. Anytime. And just so you know, unless you're blackout drunk, you shouldn't be eating at McDonald's, Burger King, Subway, Taco Bell, Wendy's . . . You know what? I'm gonna just go ahead and email you a list of places that are off-limits and I'll also include a few salad places, sushi restaurants, and coffee shops that we love. Cute?"

"Um."

"Perf! See you later." Steph smiled, turned, and walked toward the door.

"Oh! And one more thing," she added from the doorway. "You should pre-game with us tomorrow night. It's always a blast and our place is amazing. You're gonna love. My sister will pick you up at nine. Bye-eee!" she sang-spoke, turning around before I could respond.

Jonah and I stared at each other.

"I'm kinda sad that you don't wanna hang out with them anymore," Jonah said, finishing his last bite.

"They're psychos, I know. And that was ridiculous. But . . . I don't know. Last night was fun."

"You're obsessed with them," he said in disbelief.

"Yeah, in like an anthropological, ethnographical-study kinda way."

"Okay, I don't really know what you just said."

"It doesn't matter, nevermind."

Jonah slurped the remains of his drink and started to stand up. "Whatever, I'm gonna go for a run, you wanna come?"

"No running for me. My knees are still a mess, plus I have to head to the library to do some research for a paper about current female heads of industry."

"That sounds horrible."

"It's not as bad as it sounds."

"Yes it is."

Jonah and I stepped out of Chick-fil-A into the sunny Friday afternoon. It was startlingly bright out.

"That's why you're not a women's studies major and I am," I told him.

"True. You're like the only women's studies major in the history of this university who is being heavily recruited by a sorority."

"I'm not being recruited. It's not a sports team."

"You know what I'm saying."

"Jonah, it was one night of stupid girly fun. I'm not gonna join, trust me."

"Alright, alright," he said, throwing his arm around me. "See you tomorrow night at the meet?"

"Of course, text me the info."

4.

I'M JUST ADVOCATING
FOR LESS DRAKE AND MORE TUPAC

After lunch, I made my way over to the library to get some work done. The Chick-fil-A is situated smack in the middle of town where all the shops and restaurants are. Students affectionately call this the River. I guess because there's a small creek that separates the town from the campus. It's actually a really picturesque, quaint town, at least during the day, when drunk kids aren't running rampant from bar to bar. Between the River and campus is the Hill, where you have all of the on-campus housing, including Lincoln Hall, where I live. Peacock Road, where all the sorority houses are, is on the opposite side of campus. The frats, however, are sprinkled throughout the residential streets by the River. CDU is a big school and it basically takes at least fifteen minutes to get anywhere.

Once on campus, I made my way across the massive mani-
cured lawn known as the Quad. I remember the first time I
walked onto it, which must have been during a family visit. I
thought that it looked eerily similar to the type of university
where they film movies about college. Today was no different.
There was a group of three boys, all sitting on their skateboards
eating fat, overspilling burritos that I'm sure they'd picked up
at the on-campus Chipotle, which was frustratingly close to the
women's studies building. "I'm just advocating for less Drake
and more Tupac," I heard one of them say as I walked past. The
lawn was sprinkled with lone sleepers. Guys and girls just casually relaxing/reading, bags tucked under their heads as pillows.

"Hey, bitch!" I heard a blond girl yell.

"Ewwww, hiii . . ." said her brunette friend who was lying on
a beach towel, in shorts and a bikini top. She was clearly joking
and she started to laugh. Luckily I was standing behind them, so
they couldn't see me watch their drama unfold.

"Why is that funny?" asked the blonde.

"Oh my God, really? Chill. I'm obviously not serious. Jesus,"
replied the brunette.

"I literally say hi to you and you start laughing at me, it's just
fucking weird and rude."

"Well, maybe I'm weird and rude right now."

"Oh okay, I'm gonna go. Enjoy your sunburn, whore." The
blonde started to walk away.

"Love you too," said the brunette.

The blond girl then turned back and said, "Oh, I meant to tell
you. Mom called and supposedly we're doing Saint Barths this
Christmas instead of Tahoe."

Oh my God. They're sisters?

"Ew," said the brunette.

"I know," agreed the blonde.

Wow.

I got on my way, passing by the Newman Fitness Center, where a group of meathead, gym-rat guys were crowded around the stairs comparing the size of their calves. One of them noticed me staring at them and cocked his head, which was gross. The entire front wall of Newman was made of glass so you could see kids working out from where I stood on the quad. I was staring right into the cardio room on the first floor.

All of the ellipticals in the cardio room were occupied by the same girl in the same outfit. I mean, they were all the same type of girl in the same type of outfit. Their tank tops may have had different bold, neon Greek letters on them, but as far as I could tell, the cardio room basically had a uniform. Kind of skinny, sort of pretty, definitely greasy. These girls looked like they spent all of their time at the gym. One of them was going so hard on the elliptical that I was worried she was going to break it or herself. She was flailing her arms and head, and I could see that she was listening to Katy Perry on her headphones because she was very clearly mouthing the words to "Firework." I'd known girls like this in high school. Gym-obsessed, but never actually in great shape. Kinda sad. Anyway. I need to get to the gym at some point, I thought.

It was Friday, which meant most kids didn't have class and student-run clubs/organizations were given permission to plant themselves and their pamphlet-laden fold-out tables all across the brick walkways that divided the Quad into separate lawns.

I guess it was their job to heckle people as they walked by on their way to class or lunch or wherever they were going. Some girl from an a cappella singing group tried to get my attention by waving frantically and rushing toward me, but thankfully my phone rang just as I locked eyes with her. I saw that it was my parents calling, and I'd never been so happy to have them call me in my life.

"Yesssssssss?" I answered, shining a huge, fake "sorry" smile at the girl, who frowned and spun back around.

"Well, hello," my dad said, "I'm glad I caught you. Let me go grab your mother."

I could hear him putting the phone down and then the muffled sounds of him yelling upstairs to my mom.

"SUSAN?"

There was a pause.

"SUE!"

"Yesss?" I heard her say in the background.

"Come down. Your daughter is on the phone!"

"WHICH ONE?"

"The nice one."

Next I heard the sound of my dad trying to put the phone on speaker. He fumbled with the buttons. Beep. Beep. Beeeeeep. Beep. They are literally both so dumb sometimes.

"Dad?! Please."

"Hi, Tay. Can you hear us? We're both on now."

"Hi, Mom."

"I'm so glad we caught you. I know how busy you are."

"It's fine, Mom. How are you guys?"

"We're fine, honey," said my dad. "Just pluggin' away. Your

mom is taking a cooking class about autumn soups and stews. So we've been eating a lot of soups and stews."

"And chowders. Your father and I made a fabulous Peruvian corn chowder," my mom added.

"That sounds exciting and yummy."

"How are you, pumpkin? How are classes? How's your roommate? She's so small."

"Pretty good on all fronts, team."

"Great. You're eating enough? How's Jonah?" My mom asked.

"Jonah's great. Thanks for asking. It's been nice to have him here with me."

"How's it going for him?" my dad inquired. "Has he had any luck being himself in the real world?"

"Dad, Jonah's pretty open about being gay, but he's not, like, shouting it from the rooftops."

"Well, I know it can be hard out there for members of the LGBT community," my father said, as if he was proud to even know that term. I guess this was his way of showing that he cared about Jonah. It made me smile.

"Jonah's really good, guys."

"That's wonderful. Any new friends?"

I wasn't sure whether I wanted to mention my special evening with the girls of Beta Zeta. But because of my mom's history there, I figured she'd be happy I'd at least met them. Maybe she'd just be shocked, considering all the horrible things I used to say about Kelly's sunny sororified disposition when she'd come home from school for holidays.

"Yeah . . . I mean, sure. I've met some fun new people. I randomly hung out with a bunch of the girls from Beta Zeta last night."

"WHAT?! That's so great!" my mother screamed.

"Calm down, Mom."

"Okay. Fine." She was not calm. "How was it? Did you love them? Did they love you? Are you pledging?"

"I'm not pledging. I'm not joining a sorority. We've literally been over this four thousand times. I just met them at a party and they were all nice and that was it. Please don't make a bigger deal out of this than it is."

"Totally get it," my dad chimed in.

"Thanks, Dad."

"I'm just happy you got a glimpse. It's all very hard to understand when you are not involved. That's all. I don't want you to miss out on friendships that will last you a lifetime."

"I'm sure I will make great friends here without joining a sorority. There are other ways to meet people."

"I'm sure that's true," my dad added. "Okay, well, good then. Have fun and be safe, beautiful."

"I will, Dad. Love you guys."

"We love you too . . . Oh, also, speaking of Beta Zeta," my mother interjected, "you should know that we talked to Kelly last night—"

"And she's coming home for Christmas," I interrupted. "I know, Mom. She emailed me. That's great."

"Oh."

I could hear the disappointment in my mom's voice. She loves to be the one to break news about anything going on with the family. She lives for it. I actually felt kind of bad for ruining her moment. Normally I would have pretended not to know about Kelly coming home.

"Well, anyway," my mom continued, "Jessica is trying to come too. Depends on Matt's rotation at the hospital. They're so busy, those two. It would be nice to have all of you girls home for the holidays this year."

"That would be great, Mom. Bye."

After I hung up I asked myself if it really would be nice to be home for Christmas with my family. I have the type of family that likes to be in each other's business as much as possible, so being away from them had been a refreshing, clean start. Don't get me wrong: I think my parents are pretty cool as far as parents go. My sisters are older but have always made a good effort to visit me at home, so we have a closeness that I treasure, but I didn't necessarily miss any of them.

Jess, the oldest, was arguably my favorite. She was tall, confident, and always genuinely sweet. Some people are just happy—she was one of them. She always made sure I was well taken care of when I was a kid, but now she had her own life: she'd been dating the same guy, Matt, a medical resident, since her senior year of CDU. Between her job in PR, Matt's crazy schedule, and the fact that they lived in New York City, I kind of doubted that she'd be home for the holidays. Kelly, the middle Bell daughter, was not so much what I would describe as sweet. She was wild, opinionated, and a bit rough. She always knew how to have a good time, wasn't afraid to ask for what she wanted, and normally found a way to get it.

My phone buzzed again—a number I didn't recognize.

(302) XXX-XXXX 2:30PM Taylor. It's Jack. Hope it's not weird that I'm texting you. Got your number from Meg.

(302) XXX-XXXX 2:30PM I wanted to apologize if I was a dick or whatever last night. Are you feeling better? 🏢

I'd be lying if I said I wasn't happy that Jack had texted me. He was really hot, and although he had acted like an idiot after I fell, it made me feel good that he'd gone to the trouble of getting my number and checking up.

I found a sunny spot on the stairs outside of the big humanities building, waited a few minutes, and contemplated the perfect response.

Taylor 2:42PM Hey.

Jack Swanson 2:42PM Really happy you responded.

Taylor 2:42PM Did u think I wouldn't?

Jack Swanson 2:42PM Honestly wasn't sure. I was an idiot last night. Def had a few too many.

Taylor 2:43PM How are you?

Jack Swanson 2:43PM Great. You?

Taylor 2:43PM I'm good. A little sore. But good.

Jack Swanson 2:43PM I heard a rumor you're pre-gaming with some BZs tomorrow night.

Taylor 2:43PM Wow. Word travels fast. I was invited but I can't go.

Jack Swanson 2:43PM Boo. Does that mean you can't make it to the party at our house as well?

Taylor 2:44PM I'm afraid it does. I'm very important. Many CDU students are vying for my attention and I have to keep my people happy.

Jack Swanson 2:44PM LOL! Totally see how that is possible.

Taylor 2:44PM Some other time then?

Jack Swanson 2:44PM Maybe we could get together just the 2 of us.

Taylor 2:44PM K

Jack Swanson 2:45PM Dinner? Movie? Walk? Museum? Carnival? Canoe trip? Ice skating? Yoga?

Taylor 2:45PM Yoga? Really?

Jack Swanson 2:45PM Not my first choice but I'd be down.

Taylor 2:45PM Haha let me think about it.

Jack Swanson 2:45PM Tell me what works.

Taylor 2:45PM Have fun at your party tonight.

Jack Swanson 2:45PM I'll try.

I couldn't help but smile. It's amazing how a few good texts can improve your relationship with the entire world.

5.

"SICK" AS IN "FUN"

The following night I was finally feeling human again. I'd spent most of my Saturday reading/sleeping in bed and was starting to feel a little stir crazy. I was excited to go see Jonah compete. The plan was to go over to his swim buddy's place afterward to play drinking games. I was midway through brushing my teeth in the girls' bathroom, still in sweatshorts and a bra, when my phone buzzed on the edge of the sink. It was a text from another number I didn't recognize.

302-XXX-XXXX 8:39PM Hi! It's Olivia. Got your number from Meg. I'm coming to pick you up in like 10 minutes.

Taylor 8:40PM Wait, what? I can't come. I have a thing.

302-XXX-XXXX 8:40PM K.

I continued to get ready, threw on one of my favorite dresses—a vintage baby-blue shirtdress with a tie around the waist, a navy cardigan, and a pair of white Chucks, and managed to sweep on some blush and mascara. I looked fine. Not amazing, but that was okay. As I was about to walk out, checking my hair once more in the mirror, I got another text.

302-XXX-XXXX 8:58PM Hey cute tits. It's Stephanie, I'm here to pick you up instead because my sister is being a cunt so come down and get in the car. White Lexus.

I went downstairs to the front of my building and sure enough, there was Steph in the car, smiling.

"Hey! Did you get cuter or were you this cute the other night?" Steph asked as soon as I was in earshot.

"Hey, sorry. I actually have plans to go see my best friend swim tonight at Newman. I told Olivia I wasn't gonna be able—"

"Well, it's great that you want to go do that, but college is about having fun and you are coming with me. Your friend will understand."

I had no idea what to do. I didn't realize it at the time, but this was kind of a crossroads moment.

I got in.

"I feel weird about calling my sister a cunt just now via text," Stephanie said.

"Oh, it's okay," I said, closing the passenger door. Her car smelled like Axe body spray.

"I don't really think she's a cunt," she reassured me.

"Seriously, I don't care. I won't mention it."

"Yeah, def don't mention it to anyone, ever. Olivia loathes

being called a cunt. It's like her personal 'n-word,'" she said, rolling her window down and lighting a cigarette.

"Okay, I won't." I could feel her smiling in my direction, but it felt like it would make things even more awkward to look at her.

"So . . ."

"Sorry we needed to pick you up so early. We wanted to grab you before my blood alcohol level became an issue."

"I honestly had no idea that you were coming to get me, so it's fine."

"Anyways," Stephanie said as she stepped on the gas and zoomed away from Lincoln Hall toward the River, "tonight should be sick."

"Sick as in fun or sick as in gross?" I asked.

"Sick as in fun, obvi," she said turning up the volume on the stereo. The song was either Chris Brown or Ne-Yo, I couldn't tell which. Stephanie sped through the winding roads that lead off campus with the precision of a professional driver. She barely had her eyes on the road between talking to me and texting, and yet I felt completely safe with her behind the wheel. Maybe she was on Adderall. Probably.

The two of us fumbled through some pretty mundane yet varied topics of convo (e.g., sports bras, Kate Upton's ass), until we got down the River and Steph said dryly, "Oh, balls. I forgot to offer you a drink, how very poor of me. Here, have some." She pulled a baby bottle out of a huge purple Longchamp bag that sat between us.

"Hmmmm, okay . . ." I said, taking the bottle and examining it. "What's in it?"

"Fun stuff."

I didn't know what else to do but giggle. "Can you be slightly more specific?" I asked.

"Just a little Red Bull."

"That's it? Why is it in this bottle?"

". . . and a little crushed-up Xanax." She smirked and lit another cigarette.

"Xanax?" Wow, she totally wasn't on Adderall. I was way off.

"It's just a little mood enhancer, it's a nice base for whatever else may come your way tonight. No presh, my wholesome upbringing mandates that I at least offer you some, that's all." She smirked again, the same exact smirk. She must've practiced that a lot at some point in middle school. I wondered if the twins ever did pageants.

"I don't know . . ." I hesitated. The only time I'd ever taken Xanax was when I had a little anxiety attack on a family trip to Spain and thought I'd lost my passport. I knew that a small amount wouldn't do much and I also felt like I could trust Stephanie for some reason. Maybe her driving prowess convinced me that she knew how to handle extreme experiences and she wouldn't lead me astray. I thought about what my mom would say if she was sitting in the backseat of the Lexus at that moment, then immediately wiped that visual from my mind because it was weirding me out.

"Fuck it," I said, cautiously squirting a shot of the drink into my mouth. It tasted like Red Bull and NyQuil. "I guess there's no harm in pre-gaming before the pre-game," I said, putting the bottle in a cup holder in the dashboard.

"Cute," said Stephanie as she handed me her cigarette, offering me a puff.

"Oh, I don't smoke, but thanks."

She threw the cigarette out of the cracked window. "Neither do I."

Stephanie and Olivia's place was the back apartment of a beautiful three-story, white-brick, ivy-covered building with an enormous front porch and awning. As we walked toward the front door Stephanie told me that their parents chose this particular apartment because it felt secure from "rapists and campus molesters." I just nodded and smiled. I also noticed that Stephanie was barefoot.

The decor of the apartment was shabby chic gone overboard. I have absolutely no right to judge anyone's taste in interior decorating, but Jesus. I'd never seen so many tasseled lamps, floral patterns, and professional family photos in my life. The twins also had two pugs named Lolita and Lolito, whom they affectionately called "Lita" and "Lito," which seemed super grown-up for two college girls.

As soon as we walked through the door, Steph beelined to the kitchen, and I heard someone scream "TAY!" from down the hallway.

It was Meg. She was wearing BZ sweatpants, a BZ hoodie, and a full face of makeup, and her hair had clearly been blown out professionally within the last two hours.

"Hey, Meg," I said. It was actually nice to see her.

"Was Steph nice to you? She's been in a weird mood because

Olivia's been in a weird mood. The two of them share a psyche, I swear."

"She was great. Got me here safe and sound. But my best friend, Jonah, has a swim meet like right now. He's gonna kill me."

"That sexy little fucker will toooootally understand. There will be a hundred swim meets to go to!" She grabbed me by the hand. "And just so you know, this outfit I'm wearing is only fine because I'm indoors, but you can't walk outside with letters on your shirt and letters on your pants. It's called 'double lettering' and makes you look like a tard. Also, stitched letters are basically seen as way more formal, so if you're wearing a stitched letter shirt your makeup better be done and you better be wearing nice jeans or leggings that look good. No sweats. Plain PR shirts you can be more casual in, but you still shouldn't look like shit. Got it?"

"I mean . . . no?"

"Cute. You'll get a care package when you get your official bid. The girls are out back on the patio, I'm just going to go pee. I'll meet you out there."

"Okay . . ." I started walking down the hall, which was lined with photos from BZ events. It hit me that these girls one-hundred-percent thought I was planning on pledging.

"Just turn left at the end and follow the sweet sounds of sisterly love," Meg called out just before shutting the bathroom door.

I muttered a quiet "Thanks . . ." and followed her directions. There were about five girls out back, sitting around a big table drinking from huge wineglasses. I had already met

most of them (Olivia, Colette, and Sabrina), but the other two
didn't look familiar. I must've been standing awkwardly in the
doorway because when Colette realized I was there, she started
laughing, offering me a pout as if to say, "You look lost and
pathetic."

"Come here," Colette said, beckoning me over to the group.
As I got closer, I realized that there was another group of maybe
five girls around the corner, sharing what looked like a blunt.

"That's our pot-smoking contingent. I didn't vote for them,"
she said, standing and kissing me on the cheek as she handed me
a wineglass. "Drink up, the Omega Sig boys want us there early
tonight for some reason."

They were going to Omega Sig. That's right, Jack had mentioned there was another party tonight.

"Hey," I said turning to Olivia, "thanks for having me over.
Your place is really cute."

Olivia smiled brightly. "Of course. Sorry I was a cunt and
couldn't get my shit together to pick you up."

"Oh, no worries." I smiled back. Maybe this wouldn't be so
bad.

"I took a shower, drank some milk, and feel like a totally
refreshed woman now. So, let's fucking party because this week
rode me hard . . . without a condom."

"Oh, please," Stephanie chimed, appearing behind me with
wineglass in hand. "You had, like, one class. We didn't do anything this week besides drink, go back home for Dad's tennis
tournament, and drink."

Olivia made an "oops" face that slid effortlessly back into
her perfect grin as she held up her glass for a toast. "Here's to

another year of craziness, boys, positive mental health, and negative STD tests!"

"What the fuck?!" Meg howled as she joined our four-way
cheers, clinking with each of us. "You are so fucking bizarre,
Olivia. I love it."

We all sat down around the table and I was introduced to
Kenadie, a really cute blond girl with a sparkling cross hanging
from a small chain around her neck, and Lauren, a big girl with
broad shoulders and her hair in a high pony. She reminded me of
the field hockey goalie from my high school. I tend to like girls
who inhabit larger bodies because they're typically less prissy
and less sensitive than the petite ones.

"Hi, I'm Taylor," I announced with a friendly wave.

Meg, who'd pulled up the seat next to mine, put her arm
around my shoulder. "Taylor is Kelly Bell's sister and she will be
a third-generation Beta Zeta, the fifth in her family. We're lucky
to have her, so be nice, lesbos."

Colette's eyes darted toward Meg. "She could be. I won't
have you sluts courting this poor girl, and there will be no dirty
rushing. Cute?"

And then the entire table replied in unison: "Crystal cute."

I nudged Meg and leaned in toward her. "What's dirty rushing?"

"According to university/Greek law, we're technically not
allowed to express interest in you during rush because technically you're supposed to meet every sorority before making your
final decision, but technically I don't really give a shit, and neither does Colette."

"Oh . . ."

"She just acts that way to keep everyone's status in line, I guess. It's for the best. Anyway!"

"Anyway," I took a sip of my drink, which despite its vessel, was definitely not white wine. "What is this?"

"Grey Goose and organic coconut water. It's vitally important to hydrate before a night out. It can save you from a trip to Planned Parenthood in the morning, so drink up."

As the words came out of Meg's mouth, Miley Cyrus's "Party in the U.S.A." came on the stereo, causing an outbreak of squeals. Jonah would just die if he saw me right now.

"So," Stephanie said to me, "what's really going on with you and Mr. Swanson?"

"You mean Jack?"

"No, Jack's dad. Yes, bitch, Jack!"

"Oh . . . I don't know. He's really hot, but I don't know," I confessed. This was about as honest an answer as I could think of.

"So, do you like him?"

I looked down. "I don't know him yet. I guess he's . . . interesting to me," I said, then looked back up at her.

"And you think he's hot?" Stephanie was not smiling. Not because she wasn't happy, but because she seemed to be thinking really hard.

"Yeah, I guess. Yeah. Yes. He's hot, but like . . ."

"What is there to know besides that?" Steph asked, cocking her head to one side.

"Besides Jack being hot?"

She nodded eagerly, "Right."

"Well . . ."

As I took a sip of my drink and looked back into Steph's

purely optimistic gaze, I wondered if she'd ever been in love for real. Then, for the tiniest little second, I wondered if Jack had.

"Hello!" she said, waving a hand in my face. "Did you OD on that Xanax juice, or are you still with me?"

"I guess I just normally like to know if a guy is an asshole before falling for him. You know?"

"I guess," she scrunched her face.

"Like, if I hadn't stuck with *The Carrie Diaries* through the prom episode, I would've never known that George was actually kind of a pompous dick."

Steph stared at me blankly.

"So . . . you're smart," she finally let out.

We both laughed. There was something about Steph that I genuinely liked. Yes, she seemed like the kind of girl who was just floating through life, but she wasn't an idiot. The dumb girls I'd known in high school weren't also sweet, they were just dumb. Steph was funny and caring and optimistic.

"Anyway," I continued vaguely, "I don't really know if anything is going on, or will go on between us ever in the future."

Meg turned toward us.

"You know that Jack and I used to date and I'm totally not over him, right? Like, what the fuck, Tay." Meg stared at me like I was some sort of swamp monster for three full seconds. Before I could have a full-blown heart attack, she broke into a huge smile. "I'm just kidding!" she guffawed. "We never dated. We fucked once, though. I think I already told you that, right?"

She hadn't.

"Yeah, I guess Jack's a really nice, super-sweet guy," Meg continued, "but I'm more into dumb jocks with massive shoulders that I can boss around twenty-four/seven."

"Whereas Jack Swanson is an actual human being," Steph stated flatly.

"Not a frombie," Meg added.

"A what?"

"A frombie. Meaning frat zombie," continued Steph. "There are tons of crazy-hot frat guys with good hair, big dicks, and nice smiles and whatever—"

"But most of them lack a soul and are total fromb-faces for suuuure," finished Meg.

It was like they all shared one brain but used their own mouths.

"So what you're saying is . . . Jack's not a frat zombie?" I asked the group.

"Right," they confirmed, in unison.

"It's almost weird because he's so hot you wouldn't expect him to be cool," said Olivia, who had just sat down next to us. "I almost want to say he's the Ryan Gosling of CDU. Is that insane?" she asked, perhaps a little too enthusiastically.

"Yeah, it's freakin' insane, but it's kinda true!" shouted a voice from behind me. It was Kenadie. She put her hands on my shoulders. "Tay-Tay, I wouldn't know firsthand, but there are a bajillion reasons why you should date Jack. One, he's not a frombie. Two, he has big ol' friendly dimples. Three, he doesn't have herpes. Four, I heard his dad was an early investor in Vita Coco . . ."

The list went on forever and all the while the other girls just gathered around me nodding, including the big girl Lauren, who came out from the apartment and sat herself directly across from me at the table and proceeded to shotgun a full can of beer in two seconds. It was actually amazing and no one batted an eye. The rest of them were really in their girly, gossipy element and I couldn't help but take the bait and fall into the trap of totally gushing to them.

"Okay," I said as coyly as I could, "we've been texting a little bit, but—"

"Taylor!" screamed Stephanie. "Why didn't you tell me that as soon as you got in the car?"

"I don't know! I didn't think it was that big of a deal. I didn't think you guys would be interested," I lied.

Before anyone could respond, Colette came over and broke up the circle.

"We're out of vodka, which means I'm gonna be bored in about five minutes, so who's coming on a liquor run with me?"

I didn't want to go.

"We'll come!" Kenadie offered, squeezing my shoulders.

I hadn't shared a small space with Colette yet, and I wasn't exactly in the mood for a barrage of backhanded compliments from a girl with virtually perfect hair. But Kenadie had already volunteered us and I didn't want to be rude.

"Have fun," said a smiling Olivia as she tossed her car keys to Colette. "Colie's a much better driver than my sister, so don't be afraid."

"I'm not afraid," I said. But I was.

Colette sped the Lexus SUV out of the twins' driveway and we were off to the Town Pump, which, according to Kenadie, was equivalent to an alcoholic's candy store. On the ride over, she regaled me with stories of growing up in an ultra-conservative Christian household in South Carolina. From the front seat, she went into detail about her father (a preacher/"her spiritual rock") and how she wasn't allowed to hang out with boys in high school because her parents were afraid she'd get pregnant. Her southern drawl made her sound like she was talking in questions, which was confusing sometimes.

"Yeah, my dad is like super protective of me? I'm his only child, so he watched over me like a hawk. Or like Jesus. Or like a hawk with Jesus's soul and my dad's face? He even had a GPS thingy installed in my car so he'd know where I was at like every damn second."

Her accent was so sweet and syrupy, I'd never heard anything like it in person.

"So, does your dad know that you're dating boys now?" I asked.

"Oh, no. I wouldn't rilly say I'm datin' exactly."

"Oh?" For whatever reason, I pegged Kenadie to be a freak-off-the-leash, ex-good-girl type of situation.

"Kenadie's a virgin, aren't you, Ken?" said Colette, making a sharp right turn into the liquor store parking lot.

"Sure am," she confirmed.

"Um, wow," I said. I was pretty shocked that any of them were virgins, especially the sex-deprived Christian belle of the bunch. As Colette pulled into an empty parking spot, her phone chimed. She looked at it and handed it to Kenadie, ordering her to "Deal with this, please."

"What's up?" Kenadie took Colette's phone and looked at the text.

"He should know I'm never gonna pay that."

"'Kay, girl, I'm handling. Jeez," she said as she typed away on Colette's iPhone and then turned back to me and winked. "I know it's hard to believe, but this good lil' Christian's front porch has never had guests over for sweet tea. Not 'til marriage."

"That's cool. I respect that," I said, unbuckling my seat belt.

"Oh, you'll wait in the car," said Colette. "They're ID-psychos and are notorious for confiscating fakes here and I'm guessing-slash-hoping you're not a twenty-one-year-old freshman?"

"Nope. I'm definitely not. And I'd like to hold on to my sister's old ID for as long as possible, so sticking in the car sounds like a great idea."

"Back in a jif, Tay-Tay," Kenadie said before slamming the passenger door. I wanted to tell her that "Tay-Tay" gave me the creeps, but she was gone before I could get the words out. As she walked away, I noticed that she had a crucifix tattooed on her lower back, which really summed up everything I knew about Kenadie.

I sat and looked out onto the huge, half-empty parking lot. I felt like a six-year-old again, waiting in the back of the car for my mom to come back from picking up the dry cleaning or a prescription or something. While I waited, I thought about what Colette had just said to me, about being older than normal college-freshman age. It was a weird thing to say. I mean, she knew exactly how old I was because she was friends with my sister. It was a whatever comment, but something about it put me off. She was pretending like she knew less about me than she did.

Before I got too deep into thinking about it, I saw the two girls coming through the sliding doors of the liquor store. Neither of them seemed to be holding any bags. And they were running, fast, toward the car.

"I FUCKING KNEW THIS WOULD HAPPEN!" Kenadie screamed as she ripped the door open, throwing herself back into the car. "OWWWWW," she let out slowly and nasally as her ass landed in the bucket of the seat. "I knew it. I fucking knew it. Goddamnit, fucking Christ."

Colette hopped up into the SUV and slammed her door. "Emergency detour" were the only words she said before turning the key and speeding out of the parking lot, nearly taking out a husky, middle-aged man in a football jersey. Kenadie's moaning continued, punctuated by the occasional wail of fuck my life or Jesus hold me now!

"Sorry, um, what's going on?" I asked, trying to sound as cool and collected as possible.

Kenadie wailed louder this time. "We are NOT talkin' about this with her." She adjusted her weight in the seat. "Ow! Damnit!" Whatever it was that was happening had something to do with her ass or her back because she hadn't stopped squirming since getting back in the car.

"It's not a big deal, Kenadie," Colette said coldly without taking her eyes off the road.

"No, Colie," Kenadie barked back.

"I'm sorry I asked. I just—" Maybe I should've kept my mouth shut.

"Her ass swallowed the beads," Colette stated plainly.

"Colette! You bitch! Ow! Are you fuckin' kidding?!" Kena-

die slammed her hand on the dashboard in an uncharacteristi-
cally genuine moment. She was pissed but also in so much pain.
I was concerned now.

"Kenadie," Colette began, swerving onto a side street, "if you
don't want people talking about the fact that you carry anal
beads around in your ass all day, then you probably shouldn't
carry anal beads around in your ass all day."

"We're not talking about this! Oh mah God! Just get me to
the friggin' ER and shut up and drive fast and just shut the fuck
up!" Kenadie shouted.

There was silence.

I could try to think of a moment in my life where I felt
more uncomfortable, but this took the cake. I wanted to know
why Kenadie was stashing beads in her butt, but I also didn't.
I glanced out the window at the cars we were passing. Colette
must've been going at least twenty above the speed limit.

I stared at the green/beige/puke-colored carpet in the hospital
waiting room. Colette hadn't said a word to me since we sat
down and it was starting to get even more awkward than before.
My phone buzzed in my hand.

Jonah 11:21PM Um. Hello?

Taylor 11:21PM Jonah! I am soooo fucking sorry. You will not
believe what my night has been but I will explain it all to you
tomorrow, I promise.

Jonah 11:22PM Weird. But fine. Are you ok.

Taylor 11:22PM Yeah, totally fine. Love you. Talk tomorrow.

Jonah 11:22PM You too.

Taylor 11:23PM How was the meet?

Jonah 11:23PM I won.

Taylor 11:24PM Yes! xx

I put my phone back into my bag and smiled at Colette.

"Kenadie only has butt sex so that she can say she's a virgin without lying," Colette said at full volume, looking at me now.

She examined her flawless manicure and continued, "So yeah, she lets guys fuck her in the ass, and performs tightening rituals during the day in order to keep things cute and fun down there, if you know what I'm saying. The rear is a whole 'nother animal. Hence the beads."

I looked at Colette blankly.

"I'm sure you're kind of like what the fuck right now, yes?"

"Yes."

"Well, good call on not asking any stupid questions in the car."

"Thanks. It didn't seem like the right time."

More silence. I smoothed my dress and wondered if this meant we wouldn't make it to the party after all. I tried not to think about what Jack was up to and how I'd gotten excited to see him. Then I had another where am I and who am I moment, which was interrupted after a minute or so by Colette turning to me.

"By the way, Taylor. You're gonna get a bid. Obviously, you can't tell anyone until it's official, but the chapter seems to be in love with you and it just makes sense. I guess some things are meant to be."

"Wow." My face started to crinkle out of some sort of weird mixture of amusement and genuine happiness. Or maybe I was just so overwhelmed by the last hour of my life that I couldn't do much besides smile and nod. I definitely didn't have any burning desire to be a part of this group of crazy girls, but the fact that they wanted me to be a part of their world felt good.

"Thanks, I'm . . . um, I'm excited."

"Good. You should be."

"I . . . am."

"Good. You should be."

"No, I totally am."

We both looked straight ahead.

"Welcome to the dark side."

6.

POSSIBLY ONE OF
THE BEST NIGHTS OF MY LIFE

In the haze of finding out that I'd officially/unofficially gotten a bid, while sitting at the university hospital, waiting for a girl who had ass beads stuck up her butthole, I had an epiphany: College is insane. Like it's actually an insane place where literally anything can happen. And I was loving it. After twenty minutes or so of silence with Colette, Kenadie came skipping out of the ER with a big grin on her face, as if nothing had happened.

"We're good to go," she chirped.

"Good," replied Colette in her driest voice. "Do you need to go back to the house now, or . . . ?"

"Nope. I'm all good. Let's go straight to Omega Sig. I'm thirsty."

"That's my girl."

On the car ride over, Kenadie explained that the doctor wasn't able to get all the beads out, because one had broken off the chain and was too far up her "poop-shoot" to retrieve without the use of a muscle relaxer. "I just looked that doc right in the eye and told him that we'd just have to wait on that. I honestly don't trust myself to not get drunk while on prescription pills. I've done it before, it was not cute, and I swore I'd never do it again. One minute you're drinkin' and feelin' loosey-goosey with two fine young gentlemen, they offer you some more oxy, and the next thing ya know, both of their you-know-whats are in your you-know-where." Then she whispered *"butthole,"* as if it needed explaining.

"It's incredibly brave of you to abstain like that," I said.

"Thank you for seeing that, Taylor. Thank you very much."

"You are very welcome."

Oh my God.

When we arrived at the Omega Sigma house, Colette led us through a side entrance. She must have texted Meg and the twins, because they were waiting at the door with a drink for each of us. We all hugged as Kenadie caught the girls up on her situation. Once we were inside the house, we gathered in the entryway for a few minutes so Meg could give us the entire rundown of the evening's events thus far.

"So basically it's a fucking shitshow down there. Rachel puked after about twelve minutes, Sabrina and Ben broke the sink in the basement bathroom, and there is so, so, so, so, so much coke tonight. Like more than there's ever been. And it's really good, which I'm not mad at."

"Cute," Colette replied.

"Oh, and that guy Rob Sherman brought his girlfriend, who is a fucking high school junior. She's annoying, completely out-of-her-head wasted, and becoming more and more naked by the minute. Something needs to be done ASAP."

"Fucking Rob," Colette said quietly. "He is such a sweet kid and his dick is huge, but if he keeps bringing kids to the adult table, it could get ugly . . . and illegal. One of you needs to simply explain to him that just because he has the emotional intelligence and maturity of an eighth grader doesn't mean he has to fuck eighth graders."

Forty-eight hours ago, I walked into the Omega Sig house for the first time, a complete outsider. This whole world was foreign to me, unknown. But now I was standing with these girls as an equal, a part of the inner workings of a community I thought I had no interest in. They liked me and I was starting to actually like them. I was no longer on the outside looking in.

Meg led us farther into the house and up some stairs that I hadn't seen at the last party. The group continued down a long hallway that led to another set of stairs, guarded by a huge dude who must have been an OS brother. He waved us through. Before entering, Meg turned to us all and said: "We shall steadfastly love each other. And also, don't do too much coke."

The door led to a huge wooden balcony overlooking the backyard of the house. Arcade Fire was blasting, and there were tiki torches, a full bar, and a view of the whole campus. The energy was incredible. There were probably about sixty or so people hanging out and drinking. I quickly scanned the crowd to see if Jack was there, but didn't see him.

"Tell me you don't love this!" Olivia yelled into my ear.

"Yeah. This is awesome. Is it always like this?"

Olivia just smiled back at me, winked, and walked away. Someone tapped me on the shoulder and I found myself looking right into Jack's beautiful blue eyes.

"Hi," I offered, trying not to smile, but I wanted to.

"Hey. You finally made it."

"I did."

"You look great."

"Thanks, I tried."

"You guys get lost on the way?"

"Um . . . last-minute hospital detour for a girl in need."

"Sounds fun. Everyone live?"

"Oh yeah. NBD." I shrugged.

"Good." He took a swig from the red cup in his hand. "A sister in need is a sister indeed."

"Or whatever."

We both laughed.

"I unfortunately can't stay up here because I'm presiding over the beer pong tournament in the basement. But I wanted to come up and see you for a sec while I had the chance."

"I'm glad you did."

Jack leaned in and gave me a short but conscious kiss on the cheek.

"So, are we still on for dinner Tuesday?" he asked with his sly smile.

"What are you talking about?"

"I thought we made plans for Tuesday?"

"Okay, you know that we didn't. But nice try."

"Fine, fine. But we should. Come down and find me if you have a chance later."

After standing there for a minute, perplexed by the interaction Jack and I just had, I realized I must have looked very alone, so I found Meg. She was sandwiched on a couch between a couple of guys doing lines of coke off of some random girl's stomach. The girl had her shirt rolled up to the bottom of her boobs and her head hung, dangling off the edge of the wicker table. If she hadn't looked so completely content with her current position, I would've probably felt a little embarrassed for her.

I'd only done cocaine once before, on New Year's with Jonah and our friend Beth from back home, and thought it was medium fun but I never really got it. It basically just made me want to smoke cigarettes (which I don't ever want to do) and talk about my family (which I also don't ever want to do).

"Look who it is," Meg said as I sat down in an empty chair next to the couch.

"So this is where you've been?" I said.

"Want some coke?"

For some reason I wanted to do something "bad" tonight, so I obliged.

"Sure!" I said, the enthusiasm in my tone was surprising even to me, "Why not?"

Meg handed me a small plastic baggie of white powder and her set of sorority house keys on a sparkly silver BZ keychain. She motioned that I ought to dip the key into the bag, like a shovel, and then put it up to my nostril and inhale. She did this silently so as not to embarrass me in front of everyone, which I appreciated. I took a couple of sniffs, or rather "bumps," and passed it back to her; then the baggie went around the circle and then back to me. This went on for the next twenty minutes or so. I honestly didn't know how much coke to do, so I just kept partaking.

I ended up doing too much.

"So, like, the weirdest thing to me, Meg, is that, honestly, I think you're kind of an awesome person. And I'd like to think that you think I'm awesome too?"

"No, I, like, totally agree."

"You agree that you're an awesome person or that I'm an awesome person?" I lit a cigarette and inhaled. It tasted delicious.

"No, bitch! I agree that you're an awesome person and I'm, like, so glad that we finally met each other."

"Oh, good, good. Me too. Do you want a drag?" I handed her the Marlboro Light.

Meg took a long drag and looked around the balcony, surveying the scene. Everyone had gone back in the house, so Meg and I shared the couch and the cigarette.

"I never wanted to be in a sorority," I blurted out.

"I know, babe."

"I still kind of don't."

"I know, babe."

"Is that bad to say?"

"No, not at all. You think I don't fucking know that about you? You're different."

"I know you didn't mean that as a compliment, but I'm gonna take it as a compliment because I think that's actually, like, a really nice thing to say to someone."

"But sometimes we can see BZ qualities in a girl before she can see them in herself," Meg said. "We knew that we needed to continue the legacy and when we saw you and talked to you we just went in. We went in hard because we had to have you. It's actually really fucking simple."

"And I really appreciate that you guys did that, and I totally get why, but honestly I don't know what to do."

"Obviously you don't know what to do. You just got to college, there are forty million decisions to be made. It can be overwhelming. I'm overwhelmed by how overwhelming it must be for you."

"Exactly. You get it."

"I do," Meg said, putting out the cigarette.

"I cannot believe I'm saying this, but I'm so glad I met you guys. Like, literally, I don't know what I'd do for friends if I hadn't come to that first party. Like, I want you guys to be my friends, you know." I could hear myself speaking but I had no control over what I was saying. And I felt fantastic.

"Duh, I know. And let me tell you what will happen if you don't rush: You'll eventually meet a fat friend, a half-Jewish/half-Asian friend, and you'll end up dating a guy named Topher who is too short for you."

"No, you're probably right."

"I know. You look hot tonight."

"So do you."

"We should probably go inside."

"I'm down."

We stood up, dusted off any couch crumbs that may have stuck to our dresses, tousled our hair, and stomped our way back into the party. We may have been fucked up, but I felt spectacular and told myself to try to remember this moment because it was one of the best nights at college yet. Possibly one of the best nights of my life. Period.

7.

COLLEG E GIRLS ARE CONSTANTLY
COMPLAINING ABOUT . . . EVERYTHING

"Honestly, I'm kinda shocked you're pledging BZ. I mean, it's great, but I'm still shocked, considering the look of disappointment on your face when I first told you I was in a fraternity."

Jack and I were on our date. The one he'd convinced me to go on. He'd picked me up in his car and took to me to Kawa Sushi, which, according to Meg, was the nicest place for a date in town.

"Believe me." I smiled. "No one expected this less than me. But I like the girls and they're nice to me. They made all of the bullshit rushing stuff so easy. I figured I would just give it a try and see what happens. This is actually pretty ugly, the more I look at it," I said, inspecting my new pledge pin.

"They're all ugly." Jack took a bite of his spicy tuna roll.

"I refuse to wear anything they gave me in that horrendous care package though."

"Not even those BZ boxer shorts? I think you'd look fine as hell in those."

"Pink is not my color."

"Well, I'm glad you pledged. Before you decided to join Beta Zeta, I was worried about our prospects as an item."

Did he just refer to *us* as an "item"?

"It rarely works," he continued, "when a frat guy and a non-sorority chick get together. Not to put, like, pressure on *this* or *us* or whatever, but at least now we can be on the same page about expectations and stuff. The BZ sisters will be a priority in your life, just like my brothers and my house are to me. That's an almost impossible concept to grasp if you're on the outside."

"I can see that."

"Fucking spicy mayo. This shit is awesome."

"This place is really nice. Thanks for bringing me here."

"I love sushi. I'm glad you do too."

"I used to get it, like, once a week with my dad during high school."

"Well, next time he's up visiting maybe we can all go together? I'd love to meet him."

I offered up a big smile. Was this guy for real or was this just his game? Maybe I needed to give Jack the benefit of the doubt. The last guy I dated in high school, Mike Feldman, thought sushi was gross and farted every time we went out to eat anywhere. Mike now works at a Brookstone and goes to community college. Not to be judgmental, but I was in a whole new league here with Jack. Maybe Jonah was right and I had gotten hotter over the summer. I definitely felt like my boobs were bigger, but the fact that I was attracting a guy like Jack gave me a sense of confidence that I'd never felt before. My sister Kelly got really sexy all of a sudden during sophomore year of college, so perhaps that was my path and this was my time. If so, I wasn't complaining.

"So how was it going to the Beta Zeta house? Was the pledge ceremony cool?"

"To be honest, it was a bit weird."

"What do you mean?"

"Well, it was my first time meeting the other pledges and they were kinda confused by who I was, and how I knew all the other sisters so well already."

"Oh yeah, I didn't think about it like that."

"Yeah, so I had to deal with that awkwardness. It was nice of them to streamline the process for me, but I definitely would've benefited from having to go through a few of the steps I got to skip. All the other girls who got bids at BZ had already bonded because they were at all the rush events and everything."

"So, were they mean?"

"No. Nothing like that. I mean, I got some looks that were less than friendly, but they had to be on their best behavior because we were all getting our pledge pins."

"Girls are so catty sometimes. I've heard some horror stories. Especially from Beta Pi, those girls are nuts."

"It's whatever. I'm not gonna psych myself out, and overall

I've felt really welcomed by the older sisters. I know they want me because I'm a legacy, but still. They seem like cool girls."

"That's cool. So, you're the fifth person in your family to be a BZ?"

"Yup."

"That's insane. We've only had a 'three gen' once in our whole fraternity history. At least at this chapter."

"I didn't realize what a big deal it was."

"It's a huge deal. I knew your sister when she went here, but I never knew she was a legacy."

"You knew Kelly?"

"Everybody knew her."

"Really?" I took a long sip of water. "That is so strange for me to think about. It's weird how you are such a different person at college than you are at home."

"That's the whole thing, isn't it? You get here and you're handed this amazing, once-in-a-lifetime opportunity to completely reinvent yourself. You can be whoever you want to be at school."

Jack was so right. That thought had been bouncing around in my head since I got here, but I hadn't been able to articulate it. Never in a million years would I have described my sister Kelly as a leader. Growing up she was always annoyed with everyone and everything, constantly complaining, and the last to offer a helping hand. But from the sense I'd gotten from the other BZ girls, she was totally respected here for being a decision maker and a boss. They all looked up to her. I felt proud to be her sister for maybe the first time ever.

"I think you're a good guy, Jack. I just wanted you to know."

"Good. I'm glad. You're not so bad yourself," Jack replied with the cutest fucking grin. He had the type of face you want to just lie in bed and look at all day. It was gross, in the best way ever.

"You're so easy to talk to. And it's never that easy to talk to people that I really like," I flirted back.

"So you're saying that you really like me?"

"Sure."

"Is this your way of flirting with me, Taylor?"

"I guess."

"I like your style. You want anything else? Dessert, maybe?"

"I'm good."

My eyes shifted down to his hands. They were good hands. I think I may have been staring.

"You're not saying much all of a sudden," Jack broke the silence.

"So, my roommate went home for the weekend . . ."

"Wow."

"What? Was that weird? Am I being too forward? You said that college is all about being who you want to be, and this is who I want to be right now."

"That's great. You're totally right. The 'wow' wasn't a bad 'wow.' It was definitely a good one."

Sitting next to Jack in his completely adorable vintage Land Rover, I was nervous and excited and anxious and ecstatic all at once. I hadn't felt this way in a long time, maybe ever, actually. When Jack parked the car, we just sat there in silence for a solid thirty seconds. We both knew what was about to happen—the connection felt almost chemical—and it was nice to pause and just enjoy the moment.

Jack turned to me.

"I can't stop smiling," I said.

He leaned in and kissed me so perfectly that I melted inside. The perfect combination of firmness and tenderness. I kissed him back, and luckily our styles meshed. It's the worst when you don't mesh well with someone's kissing style, but this wasn't one of those times, thank God. Jack slid one of his big hands behind my head and another one around my waist and it felt like he was holding every part of me. I didn't want to be sitting in a parked car anymore.

"Let's go up," I said.

"You sure?"

"Sure . . . I mean . . . definitely."

As we got out of the car, I felt my phone vibrating in my pocket. It was definitely a text. Then I felt it again. Then again. I looked and saw that they were all from Meg, but I chose not to read them. I was positive she was summoning me and the twenty other pledges to the Beta Zeta house or one of the satellite houses for some last-minute meeting or bonding exercise, but I wasn't going to be taken out of this moment. We had been warned that we needed to be on call 24/7, but it had barely been a day since we'd gotten our bids and I'd already been to the BZ house once today for a "History of Beta Zeta" lecture that lasted almost two hours. I was not about to abandon Jack when we were steps away from my bed.

"I lived at Lincoln my freshman year. A lot of good memories in this building," Jack said as we walked into my empty room.

"It could be worse. The decor is a little depressing, but the location is convenient." I put my phone on silent and threw it in my desk drawer.

"It's a real turn-on that you're a 'glass-half-full' kind of girl. Most college girls are constantly complaining about everything."

He moved in quickly and starting kissing me again, but this time with much more intensity. As we made out I slowly inched toward my bed. Jack wrapped his arms around me with his hands on my ass and lightly lifted me up, and placed me gently on the bed.

The next couple minutes were kind of perfect. We were totally in a rhythm with one another. I felt like he and I had been doing this for years, like we learned to kiss at the same kissing school. Gone was the self-conscious bullshit that usually accompanies a first hookup. I was just there, in the room, completely focused on him. My mind didn't drift once to think about whether I was wearing the right bra, or if he thought my thighs were too jiggly or if he *liked me* liked me. In fact, this was probably the first time I'd ever been with a guy and felt this level of comfort. It was really . . . interesting.

"I've been thinking about kissing you like this since the moment I saw you," Jack said, as he pulled away for a second. He was looking right into my eyes.

"I'm happy to help make your dreams a reality."

"You're so fucking sexy to me."

"So are you."

Jack got up on his knees and pulled off his shirt.

"Can I take yours off? Is that okay?"

"Yes."

Jack then leaned in and started kissing my neck and collarbone as he unbuttoned my shirt. He kissed his way down to my chest and then removed my bra with no trouble. His hair smelled so fucking good I wanted to scream. Guys are always in a fucking rush, but he was definitely not. He was taking his time and I loved it. I could feel my heart pounding through my chest. Jack must have felt it too. His head was right there. I wanted him to hear it. My whole body was gearing up for whatever he had in store.

That's when the phone rang. The landline. I didn't recognize it at first because I don't think I'd heard it ring once during my entire time at CDU. It was so jarring and loud and could not have come at a more awkward time. Who was calling me at 10:30 on a Saturday night? I hadn't given that number to anyone. Even my family called me on my cell phone.

The ringing didn't seem to have broken Jack's focus, because he continued to caress and kiss my body. I was relieved when the phone stopped because I wanted to enjoy every moment of this.

"These need to come off right now," Jack whispered as he started taking down my jeans.

"K."

Thank God I got a wax before I came to school.

What happened next can only be described in one word: nirvana. After kissing his way down my stomach, over my hips, and onto my thighs, Jack went there. When I say that he went down on me, I really mean that Jack took my whole notion of pleasure, smashed it with a steel-toed boot, and proceeded to redefine the boundaries of ecstasy. Perhaps it sounds like I'm being overly dramatic, but I'm not. I never knew what sex could really feel like, let alone oral. It was insane. Every other sexual encounter I'd had up until that moment was amateur.

When it was over I didn't know whether to laugh or cry. I was in outer space. I looked down between my legs at Jack's face and I realized that he was saying something to me. My head was floating.

"Do you need to answer that?" Jack asked.

I guess the phone had been ringing the whole time, but I was so zoned out that I hadn't heard it. Once I collected myself, pulled my underwear on, and unplugged the phone, I laid down on the bed and curled up into Jack's shoulder.

"That was really nice."

"Happy you feel that way. Some girls just want to rush into sex, you know?"

"What would you call what we just did?"

"I mean dick-in-vagina sex," he laughed. "Didn't feel like we needed to rush into that tonight."

"Okay . . . why?"

"Because I didn't want you to think that I was just one of those guys."

"One of what kind of guys?"

"A hitter and a quitter."

"But are you?"

"Very funny. I don't know. Just wanted to wait. Is that weird?"

"I like that you wanted to wait. No complaints from me."

"Well, tonight was all about making you feel good."

"What about you feeling good?"

"Next time. I actually need to get back to the house in a bit. Duty calls. Also I would check your messages. Someone just called you like eight times in a row."

Jack put his shirt on and kissed me goodbye. I grabbed my cell phone and turned it on. Fifteen texts, three voice mails, all from Colette and Meg.

By the time I got to the front door of the Beta Zeta house I was completely out of breath because, of course, my dorm was on the total opposite side of campus. I'd never run so fast in my entire life, and I hate running. I was sweating through my clothes, and scared. Colette's tone on my voice mail made it sound like something terrible had happened. She just kept repeating that I needed to get to the "fucking house" immediately, but she wasn't yelling. She was really calm. I was terrified.

I took a deep breath and slowly opened the door. I fully expected the entire house, including all the pledges, to be standing there waiting for Colette to publicly shame me. But the house was empty. Like weirdly empty. Maybe something terrible had happened. Was there some kind of emergency or accident? Were they all at the hospital? I was very confused, yet also relieved that there was no confrontation.

It was strange to be in the house alone, like I was seeing it for the first time. During rush I was barely there, and the times I was there, it was always a shitshow with, like, a thousand people there and a million things going on. So I'd never really looked at the house that closely. I'd been inside the BZ house once when my sister was a junior at CDU and living there, probably when I was a freshman in high school. I was too young to care back then.

Beautiful old furniture and a ridiculous fireplace of carved stone. They must have hired an interior designer or something, because the attention to detail was insane. Like, all the throw pillows on the couch matched the fabric on the huge draperies that hung at the sides of the large glass doors leading to the backyard. Two gigantic paintings of abstract daisies hung on the wall, framing the fireplace. They were tasteful, understated, and had been positioned in a way that allowed for the composites that were also hanging to not be so in your face.

I walked through the empty, dimly lit common room, running my fingers along the top of the soft couch. When I got to the kitchen I saw Colette sitting alone at the island with her back toward me. I froze.

"You're late," she said quietly without even turning around.

"I know. I'm sorry."

"You know, Taylor, this isn't a joke. You need to take what we do here more seriously."

"I do. I promise. I just . . ."

"You just what?" she said as she slowly turned toward me.

"I was out with Jack and we were . . . indisposed when you guys were calling me."

"Well, good for you. But your phone needs to be on every hour of every day until you are initiated. Nothing is a sure thing until we say so. Do you understand?"

"Yep."

"This time is about bonding and trust and reliability."

"I get it. My bad. This will never happen again."

"It better not. Because there is only so much leeway I can give you without other people feeling less than special."

"I don't need special treatment. I just want to be treated like everyone else."

"I'm pretty sure that's not possible and you know it. They've all gone to the bar already. I suggest you get over there ASAP and start mingling with the other girls. Before you go, however, you need to fill out this pledge information sheet that the other girls just did." She pulled a stapled packet of papers from a stack that sat on the counter in front of her, slid it to her left.

"Thanks," I said, sitting down on the stool next to Colette's. "Do you have a pen?"

She retrieved one from her bag and put it on top of the packet.

"'Kay, thanks, Colette. And sorry again. Will I see you at the bar?"

"I'll probably show up later. I need to run and do some errands off campus tonight. Some non-BZ business needs attention."

"Gotcha," I said, "well, good luck with that. And maybe I'll see you later?"

"Yeah." She stared at her phone with a look of concern. "Just leave that on the counter with the others when you're done," Colette said as she walked out of the kitchen.

"Sure," I said, feeling relieved that she was gone.

The packet only took me a few minutes to fill out. It was a series of personal questions. My favorite color, my birthday, my height, favorite band, etc. It occurred to me that Colette didn't want me there to fill out this info sheet with the other pledges; she wanted me there so that I knew BZ took precedence over my personal time from now on. I was a little surprised that she hadn't screamed at me. But then again, I couldn't really picture her raising her voice to anyone. She was too composed, too hard around the edges to lose her shit like that. But still, it all left a weird taste in my mouth. I didn't come to college to follow someone's arbitrary rules.

I never made it to the bar that night and I never heard a word about it from Colette, so I'm assuming she never made it either.

8.

SARAH

The next few weeks flew by. In between classes and studying, our pledge class was summoned to the house about every other day to do various things, which Jonah found annoying because we couldn't hang out as often. But he had endless swim practices anyway; we each had our thing.

The required BZ activities I liked: full-chapter dinners, a Tahitian-themed Sunday brunch where I won a limbo contest, and a Big/Little speed-dating night that was priceless. Things I kind of hated: liquor and beer runs, cleaning responsibilities in the house, and a few Human Dignity workshops that were just boring.

The sense I got from around campus was that we had it pretty easy at BZ. I went to coffee one day with this super-tiny girl, Sarah, whom I'd met on move-in day. She was compact and looked a little scrappy, but had this booming voice that I thought was hilarious. We weren't really that close, but she seemed funny and kept texting me about meeting up for coffee. So we met at a café on the River and swapped pledge stories. Sarah was pledging Beta Pi. She came wearing a lavender cashmere cardigan, an Hermès belt, and Tory Burch flats. I felt a little underdressed in my shorts and T-shirt.

Beta Pi was kind of known as the slutty and raunchy house, so I wasn't surprised to hear that her experience had been different from mine, but one thing she told me literally blew my mind.

Sarah explained: "One night, before a frat party at Alpha, all of us pledges were called to the house, blindfolded, and led to the basement. A table had been set up with a bunch of vodka and mixers and we were told to just hang out and have fun and wait for further instructions. After about an hour, we were all pretty tipsy and having a blast, when one of the older sisters came down and told us that we needed to get completely naked, I'm not even joking, and sit on some wooden chairs that had been set up in a row. Each chair had a piece of newspaper taped to the seat. I was confused, but all the other girls stripped down so fuckin' fast that I just went along with it. When all twenty or so of us were seated on the cold wooden chairs, a TV was wheeled out in front of the row of us. A hardcore porn video, which apparently took place in a Jiffy Lube, was then turned on and one of the seniors explained that we were not allowed to get up from our seat and come to the party until the newspaper was wet and the ink had 'printed' on our asses."

When Sarah's story finished, I realized that my jaw was hanging to the floor.

"Are you fucking serious?" I asked.

"As HPV."

"Holy shit, Sarah. That is insane! What . . . what happened?"

"I mean, we all got there. Eventually. It started off as the most humiliating thing ever, but by the end we all felt like it was a badge of honor to go up and show them our newspaper-printed ass."

"Oh my God. My house is seriously PG compared to that."

"But you guys still have to sleep with a guy from Omega Sig, right?"

"What are you talking about?"

"We have to fuck at least one guy from our partner frat, Alpha, before initiation or we don't get in, officially."

"Wait, wait, wait. So you have to 'officially' fuck some dude? To get in?" I wondered if forcing their girls to do this was even legal. I was completely speechless. I had no idea how lucky I had been with my pledge experience thus far.

"Honestly, Taylor, I really don't mind it that much. The guys in Alpha are all so hot and one of my potential Bigs told me which of the brothers were hung and which weren't. I was gonna fuck a couple of those Alpha boys anyway, so it doesn't really matter. I can't even believe you are a Beta Zeta. I never pegged you as Greek."

"Me neither."

I wanted to be able to relate to Sarah's pledge experiences, but I mean, she was sitting across the table from me talking about how she'd basically been sexually harassed. Deep down I believed that I would never be hazed, like, for real. Beta Zeta was different. It just wasn't that kind of a sorority. They weren't that type of group.

Sarah went on about a few of the guys she was considering for the "fucking assignment" and I entertained her with as much enthusiasm as I could muster while we looked at each of their Facebook profiles on her iPhone. One guy had a mohawk, so I told her not to fuck him because before I left for school, my grandmother told me never to sleep with a mohawked man and I happened to agree with the old quack on that one. Sarah argued that "Stevey" a.k.a. Mr. Mohawk was a starter on the lacrosse team, so he would raise her proverbial asking price for the rest of the semester, if not year.

As we got up and tossed our empty soy lattes into the trash, the thought crossed my mind that I was going to need to stop judging girls like Sarah for being slutty. Not that everyone was as extreme as her and Kenadie, but there was no way I'd be able to make it through even one year in this world of frombies and soiled newspaper while passing judgment on these girls. I'd go insane. I made a promise to myself then and there: Don't be a bitch, don't judge, and just enjoy the ride.

We hugged and Sarah went off on her way and I headed toward my dorm.

My phone buzzed. It was a text from Olivia.

Olivia 4:45PM Question

Taylor 4:46PM Hey, Olivia what's up

Olivia 4:46PM You're a women's studies person right?

Taylor 4:46PM Yeah

Olivia 4:46PM Cool

Olivia 4:47PM So you know about like women's lib and shit?

Taylor 4:47PM A little bit. Why?

Olivia 4:47PM I'm having a situation with this one professor of mine who I think might be objectifying me

Taylor 4:48PM Hmm. Okay. How can I help?

Taylor 4:48PM Also is it a male or female professor?

Olivia 4:40PM Male

Olivia 4:50PM He's always singling me out in lecture and saying weird shit to me after class and I can't tell if he's being sexist or if I'm just being sensitive because I think he's a creepy old loser

Olivia 4:50PM Like today he asked me to sing in front of the whole class

Olivia 4:51PM and I'm a really good singer but it was just weird that he knew that, right?

Taylor 4:52PM I don't know. It doesn't sound that weird to me.

Olivia 4:52PM Really?

Taylor 4:53PM Yeah, maybe someone mentioned it to him or something. And you're always humming

Olivia 4:53PM I am?

Taylor 4:53PM Yeah. But it's nice

Olivia 4:53PM So you don't think he was trying to embarrass me by making me sing in front of the whole class?

Taylor 4:54PM Why did he ask you to sing?

Olivia 4:54PM Because the book we're reading in his lit class is about a French singer, and I knew the song we were talking about from high school. We sang it in chamber choir

Taylor 4:54PM Did you tell him that you knew the song?

Olivia 4:54PM Yeah

Taylor 4:54PM Then that's probably how he knew you sang

Olivia 4:56PM Oh you're probably right

Olivia 4:56PM So it's not weird? You don't feel like he was embarrassing me because I'm a girl?

Taylor 4:57PM Doesn't sound like it to me

Olivia 4:57PM Okay

Olivia 4:59PM Thanks. I'm glad I asked you

Taylor 4:59PM No prob

Olivia and I never spoke of this issue again, she never brought it up and neither did I. I don't really know why she chose me to come to for advice. Her question didn't really have anything to do with women's studies, liberation, or feminism. But it made me smile. In her own Olivia way, she was confiding in me.

9.

KIND OF ADULTS

By the time the leaves on campus started falling off the trees, Jack and I were hanging out pretty much on a regular basis. We went on a few movie dates and a couple of dinners, but between schoolwork, chapter stuff, and sleep, neither of us had a ton of extra time. But when we did, we chose to spend it together. And of course, we saw each other at parties. Meg and the girls were constantly asking if Jack and I were "a thing," and despite my pretending not to know, we were definitely becoming one.

Jack 11:40PM You want to sleep over? I'm done with my shit and we could just watch a movie or whatever.

Taylor 11:40PM I want to so bad, but I still have 50 pages left to note for psych. Maybe tomorrow night?

Jack 11:40PM All good. You free Friday? I was gonna drive down to the marina where my dad keeps his boat. We could take a ride. Supposed to be nice weather.

Taylor 11:41PM Omg yeah! For sure. That sounds amazing.

Jack 11:41PM Great. Should we invite others? Could do a little private booze cruise

Taylor 11:42PM Yes, I'll ask around. Cute!

Jack 11:43PM Sounds good, I'll see if Dave is free. PS you're starting to sound like "them"

Taylor 11:43PM Oh god, do I really?

Jack 11:45PM It's cute

Taylor 11:45PM LOL ok good. See you soon, handsome

Jack 11:46PM xx

Friday couldn't have rolled around any sooner. The thought of doing anything sorority- or school-related was killing me. I needed a break, and the day trip on Jack's boat was gonna be just that. Jack invited one of his best friends and fraternity brothers, David, and told me to invite some friends. So Meg and Jonah also came along. I hadn't seen Jonah in a couple of weeks because his swim season had taken over his life. I missed him a lot and I felt like I had a lot to tell him. It was sweet that Jack wanted to hang out with my friends.

"I can't believe you grew up here. It's so beautiful."

"Looks pretty boring to me," joked Meg from the back-seat.

"Definitely a little boring, but it was fun when I was a kid."

"Well, I'm happy to be here. This makes me happy."

Once we all parked at the marina, Jack took me down to the boat to get it all set up and uncovered, while the rest of the group went to a liquor store to take care of the booze part of our cruise. Jack's family boat wasn't crazy huge or fancy, but it was beautiful. And it was nice to have a few minutes alone with him.

"A perfect Delaware fall day. Sixty and sunny," he said, helping me down the dock ladder and into the boat.

"I love this time of year. Not too cold, the light is so romantic." I snuggled up against him.

"Me too."

I helped him untie the ropes and lay out all of the cushions.

"So you, like, really know what you're doing here, don't you?"

"My dad and I had a tradition of going fishing pretty much every weekend. It's kind of the only way we know how to relate to each other. So I've spent a lot of time on this boat."

"That's super cute."

"WHO WANTS A BEER?" David (cute, short, muscular jock type) screamed from the far end of the dock.

Once we were all aboard, Jack led us out of the harbor and into the Delaware River. Jonah and David handed out cans of Natty Boh. It was weird to be out in the real world with these people. I mean, almost everything social I'd been doing over the past few months was at school. You get stuck inside the bubble at school. It's insular. But here we weren't kids anymore, we were kind of adults.

"So, Jonah. You're a swimmer. You wanna take a dip?" David said as he picked Jonah up and pretended to throw him overboard.

I guess adult wasn't exactly the right description.

"Ha! Very funny," Jonah replied, shooting me a dirty look that screamed *Why did you make me come to this?*

"Ignore him, Jonah. We all must remember that David's brain hasn't really healed since colliding with a lacrosse ball in the ninth grade."

"Thanks, Jack, but that's pretty obvious," Jonah smirked at David.

"Okay, okay. I was just horsing around. I didn't realize this was such a refined group of young adults," David chimed in. "You're right, you're right. We should just all sit here leisurely enjoying these brews . . . or, anyone wanna do SOME COKE??"

"Sure," Jonah answered immediately.

"Um, what? Are you serious Jonah?" I asked.

"Yeah. Why not? It's Friday, it's a beautiful fall day, we're on a fucking boat. What else are we supposed to be doing?"

"Yeah, Tay, what else are we supposed to be doing?" David added.

"Dave, did you really bring coke on my dad's boat?"

"Oh, I most certainly brought a lot of coke onto your dad's boat."

"I'm down," Meg added.

"The people have spoken, fine sir," David said, shrugging.

"It's fine, I guess," Jack replied while piloting.

We hadn't been on the boat more than twenty minutes, and everyone but Jack and me was high as a kite. I wasn't disappointed, necessarily, but I'd had a different vibe in mind for the boat ride. They were all getting high, drinking, being crazy, and dancing like maniacs to Daft Punk, while Jack and I just sat together in the helm chair and laughed at them. So I guess it kind of worked out for the best.

"I'm so down for a party on a boat, but these guys are too much," Jack said. Jonah was trying to teach Dave to twerk.

"Dave seems like a real winner."

"He's usually not this bad. I brought him because he never seems be able to close the deal with girls and I thought we could set him up with Meg."

"That's really sweet of you, but from the looks of it he seems more interested in Jonah than making a move on Meg."

"You may be right. Hey, they'd make a cute couple."

"I don't think Zac Efron in that fraternity movie is really Jonah's type," I said.

"To be honest, I don't know whose type he is. Why don't we anchor here for a bit and chill? I haven't even shown you the berth yet."

"Okay. That sounds cute."

Jack turned off the motor and led me down to the lower cabin. It was cozy, with a little kitchen and a tiny bedroom at the front. Finally, some real privacy.

"This is it." He sat down on the bed.

"I love it."

"Good. I love it too. I've spent a lot of time on this boat."

"Like with your family and stuff?"

"Yeah, but also alone. This was like my own private hideaway when I was in high school. I would just come here to get away from shit."

"I'm sure all the ladies in high school wanted to 'check out' your dad's boat."

"Well, honestly, no. I wasn't that smooth with the girls back then. I wish I had been. This would have been a killer spot, but it wasn't in the cards. I was a skinny, pimply geek."

"I highly doubt that."

"No. I'm being serious. When I got to college freshman year, I was five nine, and a hundred forty-five pounds. Sounds sexy, doesn't it?"

"I have a hard time believing that you weren't cute, even if you were scrawny."

"I wish I had been, but sadly, all I did here was watch old movies on VHS and read the entire Hunger Games trilogy, over and over. Are you completely turned on right now?" Jack sheepishly smiled.

"I gotta say, you're constantly surprising me. You're not the guy I thought you were . . . like . . . in a good way. A really good way."

"Did you think I was going to end up being this meathead frat brother or something?"

"Maybe at first?"

"Oh my God! I can't believe you. That's hilarious."

"Well, I don't know? I met you on, like, my second day here. I think I had a lot of wrong ideas about who everyone was and how they would act."

"Did you honestly think that an average meathead would willfully enroll in a women's studies class at eight thirty a.m. on Mondays?"

"Point taken," I said as I closed the sliding door to the bedroom and sat next to Jack on the bed.

"Never judge a frat boy by his cover."

Jack leaned in to kiss me, and as his lips touched mine, we both laid back onto the little mattress. I was so into him I couldn't contain it. It really isn't a myth—college boys actually are better/cuter/hotter than high school guys. As Jack's body rolled on top of me I wanted to scream, but I knew I had to keep it inside. If the cokeheads made their way downstairs we'd never have any alone time for the rest of the day.

"Do you have a condom?" I asked as I pulled him closer into me.

"Really? You're okay doing it in here?"

"Yes. We can just try to be quiet. So, do you have one?"

"I do."

Jack hopped up, took his wallet out, and took his shirt and pants off as I stripped down to my bra and panties in record time. He placed the condom on a little wood ledge next to the bed and jumped back on top of me. There was something about his demeanor that was so disarming. Like he was confident, but also there was a tenderness about the way his body moved that made me feel completely free with mine.

Jack kissed me all over and worked his way down to my thighs, slowly removing my underwear. I knew what was coming next and my body quivered in anticipation. My moment of ecstasy only lasted about two seconds before I heard someone scream, "MAN OVERBOARD!"

It was Jonah's voice.

"What the fuck?" I said.

We threw our clothes on and raced up to the deck to see what was going on. Meg was basically passed out/sunbathing/ not paying attention on the front of the boat, and Jonah sat toward the back. Dave had taken off his clothes and jumped into the river. It was really warm out for the fall, but the water had to be cold.

"Come on, Jonah! It's not that bad in here. I'll race you, swim star. Get in here!" Dave beckoned from the water. A very drunk and high Jonah took off his shirt and pants and jumped in.

"You two are fucking nuts!" Jack yelled. "You need to get out, now. You're gonna get hypothermia."

The boys were not listening to Jack at all. They were just horsing around, seemingly unaffected by the freezing water.

Meg got up and joined us to see what all the commotion was about.

"Are you fucking serious?" Jonah shouted, looking up at me with a huge smile.

"What?" I called back.

"Dave, are you serious right now? Where are they? Give them back, dude!" Jonah looked pretty sober all of a sudden.

"Chill out, man," Dave replied.

Jonah looked back up to the boat and explained, "Dave just pulled my boxers off. And now I'm gonna have to repay the favor."

With that Jonah disappeared under the water, for what seemed like an eternity.

"I think Dave has a little crush on Jonah," Meg said under her breath.

We all waited for Jonah to resurface. Even Dave seemed concerned that he hadn't come up for air.

"Ahhhhhhhhhhh!" Dave screamed as he was pulled completely under the water. I was literally freaking out. Within seconds Dave reemerged, followed by a victorious Jonah, who had his boxers in one hand and Dave's in the other.

"Wait, this is kind of kinky, and I'm loving it for them," Meg added.

After a few more minutes of coke-fueled horsing around, we convinced the boys to rejoin us on the boat. Coked up or not, Dave and Jonah had clearly had a moment in the water. They were freezing and complaining, but Jonah had a huge fucking grin on his face. I was really happy for him. I was happy for both of them, actually.

We all had a few more beers, Jonah and Dave warmed up, and then got into a petty argument: *Star Trek* vs. *Star Wars* vs. *Sharknado*. It was cute. We got back to the dock around 4:30, just as it was getting cold, selected the two most sober drivers (Jack and I), and drove back to campus. The night was young, and Omega Sig was throwing a huge party that we had to get back for.

10.

SHARKS IN J.CREW

"Okay y'all, let's be cute and shut the fuck up now because Colette is gon' go ahead and get tonight's show goin'," Kenadie announced from the front of the room. I grabbed a seat on the floor next to the gigantic coffee table in the center of the room. On the table sat the current issues of *Vogue, Vogue Paris, Harper's, Town & Country, Forbes,* and *The Washington Post.* All of them splayed out with the type of precision you'd be hard pressed to find even in a fancy doctor's office (and this was true every day at any given hour). Also on the table, always, were two tall glass vases. One filled with fresh white gerbera daisies and the other with green jelly beans, which we were condescendingly encouraged to enjoy if "we were into eating sugar."

Maybe I was worn out from my week of classes or maybe I was preoccupied with wondering when I'd hear from Jack next; whatever it was, I must've been wearing it on my face because when Colette asked the group if we were ready to "stop being annoying and get into this shit," she was looking right at me. I was still trying to get a read on her and that bugged me. It bugged me that I cared what she thought of me. Sometimes she'd be nice to me and other times she'd act like I wasn't in the room. I'm normally not self-conscious about pretty/bitchy girls, but Colette was different. She put me on edge. Maybe that's what she was going for?

The room fell silent.

"Alright. Silence your phones because I'm over the texting already. Yes, Meredith, that means you need to stop sexting your boyfriend." Meredith quickly shoved her phone into her bag. "Okay, I'm gonna keep this short and sweet because we're starting thirty minutes late and I needed to start drinking like two hours ago."

Colette seemed less rigid than normal. There was something vulnerable about her tonight. I realized what it was—I'd never seen her with her hair down before.

"We're gonna break down the next few days for you and then we can all get on with our super-exciting lives," she continued. "Well, us *Actives* can get on with our lives. But I'm afraid you guys aren't gonna have much of a life over the next seven days, and I genuinely apologize for that."

As if this wasn't completely unusual behavior, Colette unleashed a fat, fake smile on all of us. And she held it. Eyes wide, teeth gritted. A weird tension quickly filled the room. It was kind of awe-inspiring, bizarre, condescending, and powerful all at once.

"Okay, you guys are getting split into groups of three. You'll spend the weekend attached to your group members by the pussy, doing whatever we ask of you as a group. You will learn to love each other, learn to hate each other, and hopefully, you'll learn how to get what you want from each other."

Meg walked over to where Colette was standing. She was holding a white iPad with a green, pink, and silver Beta Zeta sticker on the back. She took over for Colette, who fell back and stood with the other Actives who were in a circle around us pledges. Like sharks eyeing their prey. Sharks in J.Crew.

"These little groups are actually of the utmost importance, and we chose them for a reason," Meg announced. "So don't go fucking everything up by trying to be sneaky and switching so that you can be with your friends or whatever. We will find out, obviously. And we will make you look and feel fat in front of everyone, obviously. Cute?"

"Crystal cute," we all responded in unison.

"Good, good, great. Okay, so here are your groups, followed by your team assignment."

She started calling out the groups. Everyone pretended to be excited with their matches. Some groups were assigned to clean the house bathrooms with a bar of soap, a cup of water, and a toothbrush. No thanks. One group was assigned to buy, boil, and peel three hundred eggs. I didn't exactly get why, but no one asked questions or batted an eye.

I, not surprisingly, was in the last group to be called.

"Last but not least, we have . . . where was I . . . oh, Jane Brandt, Leyla Johnson, and Taylor Bell. And you guys . . . will be on DD duties until Sunday morning. Cuuuuuute."

Ugh. We got DD, which meant the three of us were assigned to cart girls around from party to party, or party to apartment, or party to wherever. This was the worst option. I would've rather gotten the eggs, to be honest.

Also, this meant that we had to hang out alone at the BZ house with Nancy, the house mother. Nancy was kind of weird and socially awkward. She was always hanging out in the great room by herself, watching *Dancing with the Stars* or *The Bachelorette.*

My eyes darted across the group of girls. Leyla happened to be sitting a few girls away from me on the floor. We exchanged a smile. She was half-Japanese and had even prettier hair than Colette. Jane Brandt, a redheaded babe who reminded me of Emma Stone but less annoying, was the other pledge on my team. Jane was one of my favorites in the class, so that was a relief. I met her at one of the first events of the year. She'd asked to bum a cigarette (which I didn't have) at one of the Omega Sig parties, which turned into a kind of amazing conversation about our mutual love and respect for Gwen Stefani's ability to stay cool for so long. Neither of the girls were people I'd consider a friend yet, like Meg or even the twins. So yeah, we didn't exactly go *way* back.

"We know that things have been super crystal cute up in here lately, but this weekend is gonna be a little different. You're gonna need to earn your keep around here," Meg announced.

"Yeah!" said an overly zealous Stephanie as she walked over to join Meg at the proverbial head of our class. "We aren't gonna make you show us your vaginas or slaughter any pigs, but trust when I say that if you want to get through this with any sort of respect or dignity you will get one thing clear. We are Actives and you are pledges. Period." The Actives all took a drink from their wineglasses. Vodka and Adderall water, I assumed.

There was another moment of weird silence. Meg laughed at Stephanie and a few girls chuckled from the crowd.

"Well? Aren't you gonna fucking clap or something? This is exciting, bitchfaces," I heard Colette say from behind me. The girls erupted into a frenzy of smiles, screams, and clapping. The Actives started emptying the room and Leyla scooted over to me.

"Hi, I'm Leyla." She smiled.

"Hey. I think we've met a couple times."

"Oh, right. Sorry. I'm terrible with names."

"It's cool."

"And faces."

I couldn't tell if she was for real, so I just grinned.

"So . . . what is your name?" she asked.

"Um, Taylor."

"Jennifer?"

"Uh, Taylor," I said, trying my best not to sound like a bitch. "I'm Taylor."

"Cool, cool. You have really pretty hair."

Before I could respond, Meg was standing behind Leyla and I realized that we were some of the only girls left.

"Okay, now's the time when *we* go get wasted and live our fucking lives to the fullest," she said, "while you guys hang out, chat with your team, and wait for our drunk texts to beckon you. Love love!" She winked at me. "And make sure you find someone with a car within the next hour . . . ish! And seriously, try to *enjoy* being designated drivers for the night!" Meg flitted off toward Colette's room. Jane came walking toward Leyla and me, rolling her eyes.

Once my "teammates" and I decided that we'd use Jane's car for the night's obligations (she was the only one of us with a car, so . . . naturally), we sat around for about three hours and did what Meg told us all to do: wait. Would I have rather been in my room asleep? Yes. But was part of me somewhat excited to see these girls at their worst without having to worry about me being my worst? Another yes.

"*Dingggg dingggg!*"

My phone went off in my bag. A text from Meg. I checked the time; it was 11:35.

Meg 11:35PM Tayyyyyyyyyyyyyyyyyyyyyyyyyyyyyyyyyyyyyyyyyyyyyyyyyyy yyyy

Meg 11:35PM Tayyyyyyyyyyyyyyyyyyyyyyyyyyyyyyyyyyyyyyyyyyyyyyyyyyy

My Friday night had just started. For a few minutes, my texts weren't going through so Meg continued to text me my name with six thousand y's, which was funny for a second until it was just annoying. Finally I called her. Meg was clearly having a good time wherever she was.

"Get the fuck OFF of me, ohmigodddd, are you grinding? What year is it?! Hello? Hello?"

"Meg! It's Taylor."

"Tayyyyyyyyy—"

"You texted? Do you need a ride?"

"Yes!" she screamed into the receiver, then out to the crowd: "Guys! Are we over this? Can we go? Shots??"

"What?" I yelled back.

"Shots!!!!"

There was a noisy pause while Meg took a shot.

"OKAY YEAH, Tay. Come to Omega Sig. Text when you're outside."

"OKAY," I shouted back, "see you in like ten."

"Bring two large Pellegrinos and a bag of salt and vinegar chips because Olivia is fat," she added before hanging up.

I turned to Jane and Leyla, who were sitting on the kitchen counter, both scrolling through Instagram.

"Omega Sig. Meg. Now."

As we pulled up to the house, Meg and the twins ran up to Jane's VW Cabriolet and piled in, basically turning it into a clown car. Jane and Leyla were up front and the four of us in the teeny backseat.

"Olivia's gonna be sick," Steph announced as the doors were shut and the engine started to purr.

Jane turned to face us in the back, "Um . . ."

"No, it's fine," Steph assured us, "just drive suuuuper slow and try not to make any turns."

Jane rolled her eyes and offered an insincere "Got it," before pulling away from the house. "Where are we going?" she asked.

Meg was texting someone furiously but managed to tell Jane to take us to this bar, Bankshots, while the twins were still fidgeting around, trying to get comfortable.

Meg threw her phone in her bag. "On second look, Liv, you look fucking queasy as fuck, babe. I mean, you always look good, but your eyes are a little bit rolly-backy in your headsy."

Jane turned the corner onto Princeton Avenue. Olivia, who was half on my lap and half on her sister's, grabbed my thigh for support as we rounded the corner. Her cheeks puffed out like little balloons. This was more serious than I realized.

"Roll down the window!" I screamed toward Jane.

"What??" Jane screamed back, keeping her eyes on the road. "No screaming in my car! Please! No screaming."

"Okay, sorry! But please, Olivia is basically puking back here."

"I don't think there are windows that open back here," said a slightly amused Meg.

"No! There are no fucking windows back there. I literally just cleaned this car, oh my God. Is she sick? Should I pull over?!" Jane was freaking out.

"Guys, I'm also a little nauseous. If she vomits I'm totally gonna vomit too," Leyla said.

"Oh my God, shut UP, Leyla," Meg barked.

"Yes, ma'am."

We were cut off by a red truck. Jane slammed on the accelerator and swerved the car, whipping us all to the left. Olivia grabbed Steph's bag and a shower of puke came gushing out of her mouth like a faucet into the bag.

"Ohhhhhhhh!!!"

"Ewwwwww!!"

"What's happening?"

"Ew, sick. Ewwwww sickkkk!!"

The car burst into mayhem. Arms flying, legs pushing against mine. I would have told Jane to pull over but we were now on a busy two-lane road and pulling over wasn't really an option.

"Please, roll the windows down. Please. I'll be fine if I can just . . ." Olivia's voice trailed off.

"It's okay, Liv. We're almost there," Steph said, consoling her sister and rubbing her head. It was actually cute. Then she turned to us, "Jane, scratch what I said about going slow. I think Jenna Westerly is at Bankshots trying to suck James's dick, so I need to be there like immediately."

"Okay . . ." I could tell Jane desperately wanted to lose it, but she knew she couldn't because she was a pledge.

"'Cause legit, I will slap Jenna. I bought her an iced latte and asked her soooo nicely not to flirt with him last week at the library. Like he's the only guy. Just, please."

She looked genuinely concerned, more with the Jenna Westerly situation than the fact that her Longchamp tote was filled with vomit. Meanwhile, Olivia's cheeks were bloating again and I could tell that this time it was worse.

The next few seconds happened in slow motion, or at least that's how it seemed at the time. Unable to pull over and let

Olivia out of the car, and with no back windows to roll down, Jane's maternal instinct must've given her the brilliant idea to roll down the Cabriolet's convertible top.

So there we were, flying down the street at probably around forty-five miles an hour and down went the convertible top. Just as it passed over us in the backseat, Olivia stuck her head up into the breeze, and like a mermaid in a fountain spouting water, a stream of puke came flying out of her pursed lips. Somehow, gravity was kind to Steph, Meg, and me, because the spray's trajectory arched over the car and missed us completely. I'd never seen anything like it, and I hope I never do again.

"Okay, I feel a lot better," Olivia said, as she wiped her mouth off with the back of her hand and tried to get her shit together. "Also, I hope you girls will all accept my deepest, most sincere apology for that behavior."

"It's fine," said Meg, who had already moved on from the puke to another furious bout of texting. I was in a state of shock, as were Jane and Leyla, so the rest of the drive is blurry. All I know is we got them there.

When we picked them up from the bar an hour-ish later to drive them all home, the three girls could barely talk, they were laughing so hard. Supposedly a Jäger shot had put Olivia over the edge again, but this time she managed to find Jenna Westerly's "heinous Michael Kors knockoff" and use that as a toilet instead.

And this was just the first night of DD.

The next night, Saturday, was not exactly as raucous as the first, but it was definitely bizarre.

After five round trips from the BZ house to the Alpha house, Jane, Leyla, and I were sent to pick up two seniors (whom I didn't know too well) from an apartment party in town on Windward Street, which seemed to be the street for apartment parties. Marley Cohen, the louder of the two sisters, had texted Jane to pick her up and seemed super anxious about it. Jane said she was using words like "immediately," "dying," and "ASAP," but when Jane asked if we should call an ambulance, she responded with an "absolutely not."

When we pulled up to the curb outside of the building on Windward, Marley and Samantha (Sam) Schroeder were waiting for us, sharing a cigarette.

"I'm smoking," Marley said as she hopped in the front seat.

There was another eye roll from the queen of eye rolling, Jane, and off we went. Marley was probably the girl in the house with the most designer clothing in her wardrobe, the one who did the most drugs, and the one who was constantly flying on a private jet to somewhere overseas to visit her "boyfriend Günter." I was always intrigued by her and to be honest, never really understood her position in this particular group of girls.

She turned the music down and took a long drag from her Marlboro Menthol.

"Let's go for a little drive. I need to regroup," she slurred, "I need to get out of that party, that fucking party, that girl, this party for a sec . . ." Marley was holding herself up as if she was completely sober, yet when she opened her mouth you could pretty much tell that she was off her-ass wasted.

"What do you mean a drive? How far exactly are we going?" Jane looked dubious.

"I just . . . we're going to KFC," replied Marley, who now had her six-inch heels up on the dashboard.

"As in Kentucky Fried Chicken? Or is that a frat I don't know about yet?" Jane said.

"Yooooooouuu are so funnnnyyy!"

"I know. Okay, no problem, where's the KFC?"

"It's an hour away," said Sam, who was sitting in between Leyla and me in the backseat.

"Yeah," agreed Marley, "the only twenty-four-hour KFC is an hour away in Edgewater. Besides, no one will recognize me there, so it's the only option. Oops." She feigned a smile in Jane's general direction.

"Okay . . ." Jane huffed.

"And last I checked, you guys are supposed to drive us any-where we need to go. Do I have the correct information, orrrr . . . what?"

Jane responded by not saying anything at all, she just got on the highway, which Sam instructed her to do, and she took driv-ing orders until we got there. They were right; it was an hour at least. But they were also right about it being open at 3:15 on a Sunday morning. And not just the drive-thru.

Marley insisted that we join her and Sam inside, where we all got to witness them plow their way through an extra-large bucket of fried chicken, a side of mashed potatoes and gravy, an order of mac and cheese, and biscuits.

"You girls will realize very, very soon that other girls are actually not nice people. Like, do you get what I'm saying? I feel like no one's talking besides me here," Marley proclaimed in between bites of a chicken wing that she was dipping in gravy.

She continued, "Okay? Girls fucking suck and when you are a fortunate, pretty, nice girl like me, then it's EXTRA fucking hard to meet nice people. Like I have trust shit." She looked at Leyla, who was falling asleep in her seat. "You get it," Marley said, putting a greasy hand on Leyla's arm. I just sat there sipping on the small Diet Coke that Marley had bought for us as a "thank-you."

I guess earlier in the night, some girl from another house had called Marley skinny-fat, which she said, "was not something you should ever say to someone's face." So she was eating her feelings at KFC on a Sunday morning, washing it all down with Red Bull and vodka from a flask. That night, I made a mental note to never use the term *skinny-fat* around any of these girls.

When we got back to campus and we were a few blocks from Marley's apartment building, I saw a girl walking alone out of the corner of my eye. She looked completely hammered, almost toppling over with every step, or I should say, with every skip. She was skipping down the street, barefoot, holding her platform wedges in her hand, her hair a tousled mess. It was actually hilarious. As we drove past her, I saw her smiling face. It was Kenadie.

"Ummmmm . . ." I said under my breath as we passed her.

No one heard me over the Calvin Harris song that Jane had blasting on her car stereo. I felt bad that I didn't say something; we could've squeezed and given her a ride, I guess.

Not a very sisterly move, Taylor.

Oh well.

11.

HAVE FUN YOU GUYS!!

When my phone rang at eight the next morning, I thought I was either dead or hallucinating. But I wasn't either of those things. I was just exhausted. The (roughly) five hours of sleep I'd had in the past seventy-two hours wasn't working out. Sleep deprivation was not my thing, but duty called.

Twenty minutes later, I was standing in the driveway of the BZ house with Jane, Leyla, and Kenadie. Somehow, Leyla looked far less tired and far less bedraggled than I did. Even Jane appeared to be holding it together, at least momentarily. *God, my life would be so much easier if I was addicted to Adderall.*

Kenadie produced a sheet of paper from the back pocket of her skinny jeans and handed it to me.

"Okay, sluts, ya'll look so fucking pretty right now. But don't you dare think for one second that I won't cunt punt you if you lose this fuckin' piece of paper," Kenadie said with a severity in her voice that I didn't know she had in her.

There was no way Kenadie had gone to sleep since I'd seen her drunk/belligerent/insane, skipping home at 4:30 in the morning, so I couldn't help but marvel at how put together she seemed.

"Enjoy the next eight hours of y'all's almost fun lives," she added before walking back into the house.

"Ughh, what does it say?" Jane said as she grabbed what looked like a shopping list from my hands. Jane was over it. I mean, Jane's general disposition was normally "over it" or "almost over it," but this was extra over it. This was verge-of-tears over it. Whatever she'd been doing to appear "okay" while Kenadie was standing in front of us had vanished the second she'd walked away. Seeing her like this was sobering and it momentarily distracted me from how deeply over it I was. I knew I had to keep my shit together if we were going to get through what I hoped would be the last "bitch" task of my increasingly miserable existence as a pledge.

"It's a fucking scavenger hunt," Jane announced.

"Like on Easter?" Leyla asked.

"No, you dick, that would be an Easter egg hunt!"

"Oh . . ."

I read the note out loud.

SCAVY HUNTY!!!!!!!

TEAM TAY-TAY, J-MONEY, SEXY ASIAN LEYLA

OK miserable bitches (jk!), you're probably tired from last night, and we get it, but you're gonna have to complete the following TO-DO LIST before 6 p.m. this evening (No Cars Allowed). And please, please, please, pleeeeeeease don't forget to HAVE FUN, YOU GUYS!

1. Run to the Safeway and buy a condom and a cucumber, lube, ex-lax, and a dozen organic eggs (Please provide receipt.)

2. Completely hollow out the eggs and place them back in the carton. (Save for later)

3. Instagram a photo of all of you standing in Yardley Fountain, naked. (you can cover up nips and puss with your hands if you feel that that's necessary)

4. Go to the Alpha house. (Front door code is 6-1-7-1-0.) Each one of you has to go up to a rando and make out with him. (photo proof)

5. While you're at Alpha, retrieve Kenadie's charm bracelet that she left in Will Boyle's room on the second floor last weekend because she wants it back but she does not want to ever see that boy's acne-battleground of a swine face ever again.

6. Collect pee and cum from an Alpha brother by any means possible. You will not be judged. (please provide photo of the brother holding both "specimen" cups)

7. Return to the house with all collected items and proof.

"Well fuck," I said, almost to myself.

"I can't do this shit right now. I'm calling my mom," Leyla said quietly.

"Ley. No. We are doing this, and we're doing this together," I said. "I'm not gonna let you quit now. I'm pretty sure that Meg told me that when you get to the scavenger hunt, you're on the home stretch, so just hang in there." I put on my bravest face to encourage her. "I can hollow eggs unnaturally fast. My mom is crafty as balls so all I'll need is a safety pin and I'm good."

"Thank God," Jane said. "My mom's an alcoholic mess who doesn't know how to boil an egg let alone hollow one out. That was honestly the only item on this list that was stressing me out."

"Well, that's good then, I guess?" Leyla said, clearly confused as to what the appropriate response would be.

The three of us stood there, looking at one another.

"Well, let's do this," Jane said. "They want us to have fun, so let's fucking go have fun."

Safeway was actually hilarious. The Sunday-morning vibe at a grocery store was something I'd never experienced. Young dads with baby strollers, grandmas, and a very extensive and diverse array of obese people. We raced around and picked up the items on the list, and since nothing embarrassed Jane we nominated her to walk through the checkout counter and pay for the ridiculous items. Leyla and I stood back and watched as Jane casually and comfortably laid out the cucumber, lube, laxative, eggs, and an *Us Weekly*, which I guess she wanted for herself. A really creepy checkout guy immediately started flirting with her.

"This looks like a good time," said the clerk through his gray teeth.

"Oh yeah? What do you mean?" Jane replied with a salacious smirk.

"Jumbo cuke, lubricant. I get off in twenty or so . . ."

"Ohhhhh, right. I see. Yeah, I get what this looks like, but I'm actually into girls. So, I'm just gonna go home and lube up this huge, thick cucumber, and then I'm gonna stick it inside of me, like up to . . . here," Jane indicated nine inches with her hand, "and then my sorority sister Taylor over there," she said, now pointing to me, "is gonna insert these raw eggs into my ass one by one, while my other very hot, very vulnerable sister, Leyla, drinks this whole bottle of laxative and then shits all over my . . ."

"Okay. We've gotta go," I said, running over to Jane. "Thanks for your help, sir."

The clerk and his mullet definitely weren't as offended as they should have been. I took the bag out of his hand, grabbed Jane by the arm, and headed for the exit.

"You're a crazy person, Jane."

"They told us to have fun!"

We walked the mile back to campus and headed straight to Yardley Fountain, which was directly in the center of the Quad. The Actives had thoughtfully picked a task that involved us being naked, in arguably the most public place on campus, in November. And to make it more fun, they wanted us to post our exploits on social media. We knew there would be little to no traffic around the fountain this early on a Sunday and our plan was to wait until there was no one in sight and then strip and get the photo done in less than a minute. I'd texted Jonah and told him to meet us at the fountain so he could snap the shot of us and he'd begrudgingly accepted.

"Jonah's five minutes away," I let them know as we approached Yardley.

"Couldn't we have just asked another girl to do this?" Leyla asked.

"He's gay. Gay trumps girl in these types of situations," Jane explained. "The last thing I need is some random-ass bitch silently judging me as I stand in a freezing fucking fountain."

"Jonah's gay? I thought he was your boyfriend, Tay," Leyla said, bewildered.

"Ley, you are legit the most special girl I know. Like, there are some extra special girls in this bunch, but you're special as fuck. And I say that in the most complimentary way possible," Jane said as she starting taking her clothes off.

"Thanks," Leyla replied quietly.

"You're welcome."

"Jonah is my best gay. We went to high school together."

Jonah arrived just at that moment looking tired, angry, and annoyed, wearing a down jacket, gym shorts, socks, and Adidas sandals.

"I didn't know you were gay," Leyla blurted out.

Jonah just stared at Leyla. Without saying a word he held his hand out for me to give him my phone. We all stripped down, hopped in the water, and Jonah took a few different angles. We all tried to cover up as best we could.

While Jonah was snapping photos, I got a good glimpse of Jane's tits and they blew me away. I thought they were man-made. Like, actually, they were the best boobs, real or fake, that I'd ever seen. They sat high and perky (but not pointy) and her nipples were perfectly nickel-size. No wonder she had no issue getting naked. I really wanted to touch them just to feel what they felt like. There we were standing in the middle of the fountain at 9:30 in the morning, posing naked. *Holy shit, this is really happening.*

The pictures looked good enough, so we all threw our clothes back on. Jonah kissed us each goodbye and vanished, but not before saying, "I'd fuck all of you."

"Thanks, you're the best." I smiled. "Now go back to sleep, you look like shit."

The three of us ran back to my room to shower and warm up before heading to Alpha for the various shit we needed to complete over there. As tired as I was, and as horrible as the scavenger hunt seemed, I was kind of having fun. Leyla and Jane were keeping me entertained and I'd probably never do this type of thing again, so I figured I might as well eat it up.

I showered first then got to work on hollowing out the eggs while they got ready. Once the eggs were empty and we were all semi-presentable, we walked over to Alpha house. I knew Jane would take the lead on getting the cum and pee from an Alpha brother, but we each had to make out with one random brother. It felt weird to me because I'd just started feeling like Jack was my boyfriend. I knew he'd be fine with whatever (within reason) I had to do to complete my pledge duties. I mean, he was the one who'd said that "sometimes the chapter just has to come first," but I honestly did not feel like finding some hungover Alpha asshole and putting my tongue in his mouth.

The plan was for Leyla and me to grab the first two kissable guys we saw, snap a photo, and get out of there, while Jane snuck into Will Boyle's room and did her thing. We unlocked the front door and let ourselves in. The house was fucking sick (in a bad way). I mean, the Omega Sig house was disgusting, but compared to this shit hole, it was the Plaza Hotel. Alpha house looked and smelled like the inside of a homeless man's ass. Red cups everywhere, and overflowing trash cans populated every corner in sight. I was terrified. Not just for me, but for the future of the world.

"I'm just gonna find a guy who doesn't look like he puked on himself, and kiss him while he's sleeping," I told Leyla.

"Okay, great. Just let me know when you're ready. I'll probably just do the same."

I looked around to see what my options were. I was not impressed.

"How about this one," Leyla said, pointing to a shirtless, hairless freshman, who was passed out with his ass up on a Ping-Pong table.

"How about this one . . . for what?" boomed a strong voice from behind us.

I turned around and locked eyes with a giant of a man in nothing but a pair of gym shorts, standing in the doorway of the kitchen. Dirty blond, piercing brown eyes, sexy as fuck in a dumb-jock kind of way.

"Oh, hey. Sorry." I struggled to get the words out.

"That's fine," he replied, "but can you answer the question?"

"We, um . . . the thing is . . . um, we're pledging Beta Zeta and we have to make out with an Alpha brother for this stupid scavenger hunt thing."

"Sounds chill."

"Yeah."

"You guys should make out with me," he added.

"Really? Would that be okay?" Leyla asked.

"Yup. Both of you. Absolutely." He grinned.

Leyla and I each took a turn kissing this dude. His name was Kenny, he played on the hockey team, he was six foot seven, and he wasn't even that bad a kisser. We locked lips for a total of four seconds. I was completely relieved when it was over, because I felt nothing tingly while it was happening. Leyla, on the other hand, ended up making out with him for at least three minutes. They actually could have made a really cute couple.

As Leyla and Kenny were finishing up, Jane came running down the stairs with her T-shirt and jacket in one hand, and two red Solo cups in the other.

"We gots to go, kids," Jane said, trying to put the shirt on, but having difficulty because of the cups.

"You okay?" I asked.

"Oh, yeah. I'm fine. We're done. Got it all. Scavenger hunt complete!" Jane yelled as she rushed out the front door.

Leyla gave Kenny the hockey man a last lingering smooch on the cheek, and we sprinted out of the house to catch up with Jane.

"Holy shit that was fucking crazy!" Jane screamed.

"You got everything?" I asked.

"Will Boyle was the jackpot. Dude was dead asleep. Found Ken's shit in like ten seconds, no joke. Then kissed him, while taking a pic of us. He woke up, I told him that I'd show him my tits if he jerked off into this cup, which I did and then he did, but not before pissing into this cup. All in all took me about six minutes. You guys get what you needed?"

"Amazing. You are amazing. Yeah. We both made out with the same guy and took pics. We're done!"

We had a fun group hug, careful not to spill any of Will Boyle's fluids.

"Can we go eat?" Jane asked, "I'm fucking starving."

The three of us went to the dining hall and scarfed plates of eggs, pancakes, and bacon. And the best part was that it was only 11:30 a.m. We barely talked. We just stuffed our faces and were back at the BZ house with all of our "Scavy Hunty" items before 1:00. Fuck. Yes.

"Well, that's a house record," Colette said as we walked in the door. "Are you sure you got everything?"

"We're sure," Jane replied.

"Well, good for you. Be back here tonight at eight wearing an all-white dress with your pledge pin, nude underwear, and flats. Also, no makeup. Cute?"

"Crystal cute," we answered.

"Oh. And come sober. Seriously. You need to be here with your hearts and minds completely pure."

12.

COMPLETE SILENCE
AND TOTAL DARKNESS

*A*fter the craziness of the weekend, and all the rumors and secrecy about *sorority initiation ceremonies*, I didn't know what to expect when I came back to the house that night. I was nervous, but I'd come this far, endured so much, and spent so much time in pledge hell already that I wasn't about to drop out now.

When I walked up the front stairs, Meg was already waiting for me with what looked like my paddle, wrapped in green, pink, and silver wrapping paper.

"Open it."

"Now?"

"Yes, bitch."

I started to pull off the paper and ribbons.

"Disclaimer: I'm not naturally crafty, and wrapping this was a fucking challenge. So, sorry it looks like a blind kid with no arms wrapped it."

"It's great," I lied. "I fucking love it. You are crafty, this looks amazing. Thank you so much," I gave Meg a huge hug. The paddle was pretty much a sparkly hideous mess, but I guess all sorority paddles are, by nature.

"You can't bullshit a bullshitter." She squeezed me back.

"Well, it looks like you put a lot of effort into it, anyway."

Meg took the paddle out of my hands and threw it in a bush to the side of the stairs.

"I'll get that back to you later. We need to go inside."

I joined all of the other pledges in the backyard.

"I have to pee so bad," Jane whispered in my ear a bit too loudly. She was smiling and her eyes sat low.

"Are you drunk?" I asked Jane.

Her grin got wider across her face.

"Just hold it. I'm sure you can pee when we get inside."

Colette came out to the backyard wearing a beautiful white dress, which I think was from Alice + Olivia, and I made a mental note to try and find it online later. She looked stunning. Her hair was wrapped in a tight, high braid and around it was a crown of white daisies. She glided toward us, holding a glowing, white candle.

"We officially welcome you, the Beta Zeta Fall 2015 Pledge Class, into our home, into our lives, and into our hearts."

Colette gave us a little smile as she turned and led us back into the house. Inside, all of the lights were off and the entire chapter was standing in the dark, also wearing white dresses. Each one of them held a candle or two. Once we'd all filed into the living room, each Big approached each Little and handed her a candle. It had all been choreographed meticulously. Meg handed me my candle and ushered me into position.

All twenty-one pledges formed a circle, each with her Big standing right behind her and her Grand Big standing right behind them. Amazingly, this was all happening in complete silence. It was definitely creepy in a Tom Cruise, *Eyes Wide Shut* kind of way, but I was into it.

"We shall steadfastly love each other," Colette said, calling the initiation to order.

"We shall steadfastly love each other," we all repeated.

"Sisterhood is the foundation of our organization," Colette continued. "It is our reason for being. If you have nothing else in this life, you will always have your sisters from Beta Zeta. The commitment you make tonight will last a lifetime. You may not always agree with every sister, you may not always see eye to eye with your sisters, you may not even talk to your sisters for long periods of time throughout your life. But your sisters will always live in your hearts. Should you ever need the help of a BZ sister, no matter what the circumstance, she will always be there for you."

Then she began singing the BZ song, which we'd all been learning and practicing over the past few weeks, and we all joined in:

I have met the sweetest girl,
She's as good as one can be,

I've seen the one I'll cherish, she means the world to me,
She holds the whitest daisy,
And the silver, pink, and green,
Beta Zeta I love you,
And to you I will be true.

As we sang the song, Nancy, our house mother, who was wearing a loose linen pantsuit, placed a glass vase in the middle of us. A long table draped in a pink and green tablecloth was carried out of the kitchen by a few older sisters. Just after the table was set down, a huge coffin that had been painted silver, pink, and green, and covered in daisies, was lugged out of the kitchen by four pallbearer Actives. It was all kind of pretty, but still really scary, because it was a coffin and I had no idea what it was doing there. I could feel the room getting tense.

When the song was done, Colette stood and pointed to an object on the table that I didn't recognize.

"This is our member book. I will now call you up here individually to sign it. Once you have signed your name, your Big will hand you a daisy and remove your pledge pin. Then you will walk over to our chapter coffin, get in it, and we will close it. This will signify the death of you as an unaffiliated member. When we reopen the coffin you will be reborn as an *Active*. Your Big will then put on your member pin and help you out of the coffin. Proceed to the vase and as you place your daisy into it, please recite the Beta Zeta motto loudly and clearly. Then return to your position in the circle. Once each pledge has become an Active, we will all march out of the house and into the night, as a united sisterhood. As a family."

It took about an hour for all twenty-one of us to do the coffin thing. Some girls cried out of fear and claustrophobia, some girls laughed with excitement, and this girl Jenny fainted and had to be taken outside. It all happened in a blur. For some reason Colette saved me for last. There was no specific order that was clear to me, but I thought it was weird that she chose to call me at the very end.

"Taylor Bell."

Maybe she was sending me a message in some way. But I was trying not to read into it too much. I wanted to enjoy the moment as much as I could. I walked over to the book. It was huge and the names were tiny. As I signed my name I realized that I was the fifth woman in my family to sign her name in this exact book. This was something that we'd share forever. It was strange to think about them doing the exact thing I was doing right now. As Meg removed my pledge pin and escorted me over to the coffin, I thought about running for the door. I fucking hate small spaces, but Meg looked me in the eye and said, "It's worth it."

And then . . . complete silence and total darkness.

It felt like I was in there for an eternity. Just when I thought I couldn't take it anymore, the coffin flew open and I was free. Meg helped me out, put on my white daisy member pin, and my eyes filled with tears.

"We shall steadfastly love each other," I said as I let the daisy slip out of my hand and into the vase. And then it was over. We all filed out into the backyard, still holding our candles, no longer pledges.

We were full-fledged sisters now.

I was a full-fledged sister now.

After our initiation was over, it was time to go to the official initiation party thrown by the fine gentlemen of Omega Sig. They'd gone all out. This was by far the most intense party Jack's house had thrown yet. Still unclear as to whether that was a result of personal perception, blood alcohol content, or just plain fact, but everything about it seemed heightened to me. Dubstep versions of Ellie Goulding songs pounded throughout the OS house. It all just felt different now and not just for me. Everyone seemed to feel that way.

"You're literally my sister now!" I screamed into Meg's ear. Mouth filled with ice from the vodka cran I'd just downed.

"I know! That's like what I've been trying to tell you. I fucking hate this song."

"I mean, before it was like we were close friends and you had my back and stuff. But now . . ."

"It feels different, doesn't it?"

"Exactlyyyy." I was drunk.

"You see, this . . . this right here is what no one on the outside will ever understand. We are blood now. And blood is thicker than water."

"And vodka!"

"So whatever happens, we're in it together."

We hugged for a really long time before both breaking into laughter.

I'd lain in the same coffin as all of these girls. I'd signed my name in the same member book as generations of Beta Zetas who came before me. I was a part of something bigger than myself, and bigger than anything I'd ever been a part of.

"There's no going back now," a deep voice said from just behind me.

Jack looked amazing, smelled amazingly good, and tasted even better when he kissed me.

"I hope you didn't go to all this trouble just for me," I said to him, gesturing to the party.

"Well, that's where you're mistaken." Jack grabbed me by the waist and pulled me into his big, warm body and proceeded to sing "All for You," that Janet Jackson song.

"You shouldn't have!"

We kissed.

"What a difference a month or two can make in your life, huh?" Meg semi-awkwardly interjected. "Look at you now! You're a Beta Zeta, your tits have never looked better, and you even have a frat-boy boyfriend."

"Sorry for dry humping in your face, Meg," Jack said, still kissing me.

"It's all good," Meg replied. "We should all be celebrating our mutual love for one another."

"Are you, though?" I asked Jack.

"Am I what?"

"My boyfriend."

"Yeah, Jack. Are you?" asked Meg.

"That depends on whether or not Miss Bell wants me to be."

I'd thought of Jack as my boyfriend, but we'd never talked about it.

"Of course I do!"

"Then that's exactly what I am."

I jumped up onto Jack, wrapped my legs around him, and squeezed. I didn't give a shit. I was that girl.

"Yay! It's, like, almost creepy how much you love each other already," squawked Meg.

"I'm really fucking happy right now," I whispered into his ear.

"Me too, Tay. Me too."

13.

Y'ALL, ARE WE FIGHTING?

The next two weeks flew by as I did my best to catch up on research for papers and group projects. My life as an Active had officially begun, but unfortunately, I'd focused so much energy on Beta Zeta activities leading up to the initiation, I was buried under a mountain of schoolwork that I'd been blowing off. I wasn't in danger of failing any classes, but I also wasn't going to get that 4.0 GPA I'd had in mind when I got to school.

I had, however, agreed to be on the planning committee for the upcoming Children's Hospital Benefit, an event that the CDU Beta Zeta chapter threw annually. I was included in a group text from hell.

It began as I was leaving the women's studies building, where my head-warpingly boring female Russian lit class is held . . .

Meg 11:35AM Hello friends/bitches/sisters/planning committee! It's time to get going on the children's hospital fund-raiser. :)

Meg 11:36AM let's save these cancer kids!!

Colette 11:41AM Let's never refer to them as cancer kids again people

Meg 11:42AM sowwy

Meg 11:45AM kinda :/

Stephanie 12:04PM But for reals can we talk about our first meeting? I'm offering up our place and this weekend is looking good. Definitely need to meet before xmas break which is in less than TWO WEEKS WTF!

Stephanie 12:07PM ugh I can't believe finals are next week. I'm failing bio

Stephanie 12:08PM again

Taylor 12:10PM Hey, just seeing these. I could do this weekend, what works for people?

Olivia 12:12PM This weekend is going to be hard for me as I have eight finals next week and a thirty-page essay to finish

Olivia 12:12PM side note: is anyone else's Adderall not really working recently

Olivia 12:13PM do we have to have it our place, Steph?

Meg 12:14PM oh get off me Olivia. Can't you let yourself live for once?

Olivia 12:15PM I don't appreciate that

Meg 12:15PM 💩

Olivia 12:16PM I don't appreciate that either, Meg

Colette 12:20PM Ugh shut up please. So saturday afternoon, say 3?

Taylor 12:21PM works for me!

Jane 12:22PM me too

Meg 12:26PM LOVES IT. I'll make my guacamole

Kenadie 12:30PM Ooooh and I'll make my queso

Kenadie 12:31PM FUN!

Olivia 12:34PM Does there have to be food at every function? Jesus. No one even eats at these things

Kenadie 12:35PM I do!

Colette 12:37PM We know you do.

Meg 12:39PM Soooooooooooo just to get our head in the game a little, should we divvy up the roles before the meeting?

Stephanie 12:40PM great!

Meg 12:42PM I have the twins on guest list and invitations and was thinking that would be good for Taylor too cause you're such a legacy 😉

Taylor 12:44PM Alright

Olivia 12:45PM Can I design the invitations again, or are we just doing an ecard this year? What's the budget?

Meg 12:46PM Well I think most of the budget (which we have saved from last year) should go to the musical guest

Meg 12:46PM Jack Johnson or Ellie Goulding????!!!

Olivia 12:49PM What's the budget for the event?

Meg 12:50PM Liv are you being a cunt?

Olivia 12:51PM I am not meg. Am I?

Meg 12:52PM It certainly seems that way. But sometimes I can't tell if you're being a cunt or you're just being your normal self

Olivia 12:55PM So you're saying I just AM a cunt?

Olivia 12:56PM all the time?

Meg 12:57PM I'm not not saying that

Colette 12:59PM No one has time for this shit

Stephanie 1:02PM Yea I don't

Kenadie 1:03PM Y'all

Stephanie 1:04PM Get your shit together you guys

Kenadie 1:08PM Y'all are we fighting?

Jane 1:11PM Did any of you see my iPad at the house?

Kenadie 1:15PM I hate it when we fight! This should be about the cancer kids! Can we not put our differences aside. Olivia needs space to study y'all, we need to respect that, so why don't we have the meeting this wknd at mine?? I'll make my dead Meemaw's deviled eggs. Colette I know you love them eggs 🎉 🎈 🎉 🎈

Olivia 1:17PM Ew

Stephanie 1:18PM Ew

Taylor 1:18PM I actually really like deviled eggs, ken

Colette 1:18PM FUCK YOU Kenadie

Meg 1:19PM Ew

Kenadie 1:20PM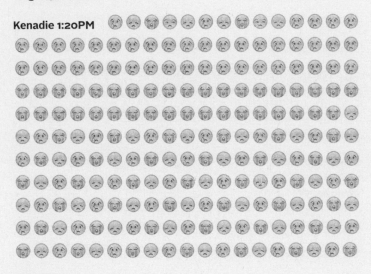

Meg 1:37PM omg

Colette 1:41PM OKAY

Stephanie 1:41PM I'm gonna pretend that didn't just happen. I thought you took control over your excessive emoji problem??? Didn't you see a therapist last year about it Kensicles?

Stephanie 1:42PM like that wasn't cool

Meg 1:43PM Yea that was way too many emojis

Meg 1:43PM I'm scarred by how many emoji faces I just saw

Colette 1:45PM WE WILL BE HAVING THE MEETING AT STEPH AND LIV'S ON SAT AT 3

Meg 1:47PM Okay

Taylor 1:47PM Alright cool

Stephanie 1:48PM I'll make sure there's fun stuff to drink

Stephanie 1:50PM Liv, I'll have Hailey come take meeting notes for you if you're TOO SMART and STUDIOUS to make it

Olivia 2:01PM No it's fine whatever

Olivia 2:01PM I'll be there

Kenadie 2:04PM Y'all I'm sorry. I woke up and snorted a bunch of ritalin this morning for some reason

Kenadie 2:04PM Won't happen again

Colette 2:05PM No it won't. This event needs to be fucking flawless

Kenadie 2:07PM Yes ma'am

Jane 2:08PM I'll be there sat @ 3

Jane 2:08PM but seriously has anyone seen a white iPad with a blue leather cover thingy at the house? It has a super important presentation on it that I need for psych tomorrow

Meg 2:11PM No Jane no one's seen your fuckin iPad

Stephanie 2:12PM No fighting!

Stephanie 2:12PM I can't with you whores right now, jesus

Leyla 2:20PM Hey guys just seeing these was at the gym

Leyla 2:21PM Whasssssssssup???!!!

14.

SISTERLY LOVE

The Children's Hospital Benefit meeting never happened because Colette's mom's Pomeranian was hit by a car, and she had to rush home to be with her for moral support. Colette clearly didn't trust the rest of us that much, because she didn't want the meeting to happen without her. Finals, however, did happen. Honestly, they weren't half as bad as I thought they'd be. Turns out high school is ten times harder than college.

I coasted through my exams, said my goodbyes to Jack (we had sex and he lent me one of his sweatshirts to wear home, which was super cute), bid the BZ girls farewell (probably the most hugging I've ever done in a twenty-minute period), and then hopped in the car with Jonah and headed home to McLean.

The summer before college, I was so excited to get out of there, but I distinctly remember thinking how nice it would be to come back home for winter break and see all my old friends. Now that it was here, I couldn't imagine having ever felt that way. I got a few texts from some kids I went to high school with, and I pretended to be excited to see them and catch up, but the truth was that I didn't really have the desire to do any such thing. Without me realizing it, my life had evolved into something else and being home felt like a step in the wrong direction. I missed school, I missed Jack, and I missed the BZ girls.

I spent the week before Christmas hanging out with Jonah, eating all the amazing food my parents cooked for us, and catching up on all the *Real Housewives* episodes I'd missed when I was at school.

Kelly got home on Christmas Eve.

"Hey, Kel," I said as she walked into the kitchen, where I was perched at the counter eating half a grapefruit and a yogurt. Being at home really was all about when and what I was eating.

Kelly looked strangely glowy and fresh, considering she'd just gotten off of a long flight from Zambia. That was the thing about my sister; she always looked amazing. Though she was less tan than I expected her to be.

"Hey, babe. How are you?" Kelly said as she dropped her bags by the door and came in for a huge hug. *Odd, Kelly isn't much of a hugger.*

"Fine. Bored. The past week in this house has been riveting," I whispered just as our dad walked in behind Kelly through the door from the garage.

"Two out of three in the same house. Not too bad. Not too bad at all," he said as he roughly hugged us, giving us each a kiss on the top of our heads.

"Dad, we did this whole bit at the airport. Enough," Kelly protested while inside of our family group hug. *Ah, there's the Kel I know and love.*

"So rude of Jessica not to be here for my triumphant return."

"Right?" I added.

"Well, do me a favor," my dad interjected, "don't mention it around your mother. She's upset enough about Jess not being here. The last thing she needs is to feel like you guys are too."

"Well, Dad, I am upset about it," Kelly said. "And who does this Matt character think he is anyway, asking Jess to marry him without getting my permission? It's rude. It's just not proper." Kelly flung the refrigerator door open, "Jesus. Is there any coconut water in this godforsaken home?"

"Well, Matthew did ask me, and I'm pretty sure that's the standard custom, so . . ." my dad added. "I'm going upstairs to finish my episode of *Game of Thrones*."

"You watch that crap, Dad?" I asked.

"Yeah. So?"

"It's like dragons and midgets and stuff," said Kelly, still looking through the contents of our parents' fully stocked fridge.

"Yeah?"

"That's all I'm saying."

"Okay . . ."

"Bye, Dad."

My dad disappeared up the stairs.

"You can't choose your family, but you can choose not to be around them," Kelly said with a smile. "Wanna help me unpack?"

I just smiled back. I didn't exactly feel like helping anyone do anything at that moment, but I knew that Kelly really meant she wanted to hang out. I wanted to hang out with her too. We'd emailed and Skyped a handful of times while she was away, but obviously I'd been busy at school and she had her own responsibilities with the internship, so we hadn't properly caught up. Not to mention that she'd been seven thousand miles away with limited Internet access. For the first time maybe ever, we had a lot to talk about. So up to her room with all of her shit we went.

"OH MY GOD, I'm so fucking happy to be home right now," Kelly said, flopping face-first onto her bed.

"I'm over it already, but I guess if I'd been in Africa for the past six months I'd feel differently." I laid down next to her.

"Yeah. I don't know."

"Kel, I'm really proud of you for doing the internship. I wasn't sure how you'd handle living in a developing nation, honestly. But you totally did and I think it's amazing."

"It wasn't that big a deal. It went really fast."

"Yes, it is a big deal. You helped people who don't have as much as we do. You made modern medicine readily available to them. Are you kidding me?"

"Um, okay. Enough about my boring life. Tell me what's been going on with you. Can you please tell me, in detail, how my hippie, women's lib, completely anti-Greek sister ended up rushing Beta Zeta?"

"Jack."

"What? Who?"

"In a word: Jack. That's kind of how I ended up meeting the girls and rushing."

"Swanson?"

"Yes."

"Oh my God. I'm jealous."

"Ew!"

"So . . . how did that pan out?"

"I mean, it's been almost three months and we're still together. I think he likes me."

"Duh," she said, "I can see it. He's fucking hot and always seemed like a really nice guy."

"So, you have no horrible dirt on him that I need to know immediately?"

"I got nothing," Kelly admitted.

"Good! I mean it's not like I thought you would, but I'm still relieved to hear that my instincts were right."

"So, what? You thought that you had to join a sorority to get him to like you?"

"Not at all. I fell for Jack, but I also fell for the girls in the chapter. I'm making a lot of good friends."

I continued to walk Kelly through all the steps that led to me loving the girls and ultimately pledging. Telling her my story was kind of amazing—partly because the fall semester had been such a whirlwind that it was fun for me to talk it through and process it all. But also because it was probably the first conversation that I'd ever had with Kelly where I felt like we were speaking the same language.

"So, you just pretty much skipped rush altogether? Jesus, they dirty rushed the shit out of you," Kelly said, pushing a stack of T-shirts into a drawer. "That's fucking insane. The chapter could get so much heat from the Panhel for pulling that shit."

"Well, they drove a hard bargain, and when they came to my rescue me after I fell at that first Omega Sig party . . . it really made a big difference."

"But still, I told Colette that there was no way in Hades you were even a pursuable option when you got accepted last year. I'm surprised they even approached you at all."

"Well, I was at a frat party looking pretty cute."

"Because of Jack."

"True."

"I'm just still in shock. Was Colette there when you were approached?"

"Meg was the first one to come up to me. She's an acquired taste but I've learned to love her."

"Okay . . . When I was away I didn't really think about it too much. But now that I'm sitting here with you, I kind of get it and it kind of freaks me out."

"We shall steadfastly love each other."

"Wowwww. You're really buying into the sisterly love over there."

I laughed at myself. "Hey, I'm still the same Taylor who thinks the whole thing is pretty silly, but now I'm just more willing to try things I'd never done before."

"So being in a sorority has made you less judgmental, how is that possible?"

"I always assumed that you and Jess and all of your cute little friends in cute little dresses just joined a house to meet guys, get drunk, and have fun. But the friendships I've made, the work the chapter does with the children's hospital, the bonds people have with each other, and the loyalty is really fucking cool. I mean, do you honestly think you would've gotten on a plane the day after graduation to go help people in Africa if you'd never been a BZ?"

"You're right. I one-hundred-percent would not have."

"Yes. I am right. It's a good organization."

"Well, damn," she said, leaning back and looking up at the ceiling. "I guess it's nice to hear you say that about Beta Zeta. Fucking insane that it's coming out of your mouth, but still. I'm gonna lay down for a few minutes . . . slash twenty-four hours."

"Okay, do it. Love you. Get some rest," I said and got up from her bed.

"Hey, Tay," Kelly stopped me before shutting her bedroom door behind me, "I know you're fucking in it right now. And the girls have brought you in under their wing, but just be careful."

"Oh . . . kay."

"I'm just saying that sometimes the excitement of the whole Greek world can be intoxicating. Not everyone in that house has the house's best interests in mind. It's like with anything else, girls will do whatever it takes to get to the top and stay there. I just don't want you to lose your good judgment of people. You were always really good at trusting your instincts."

"So what are you saying?"

"Just don't forget who you were before you pledged. That's it. Really."

"I won't. I promise."

Kelly raised her eyebrows.

"I fucking promise you that I won't let those bitches change me, okay?"

"'Kay, see you in a bit."

"Sleep well, Kelly."

I shut her door and went into my room, which, by comparison to Kelly's, was still pristine and untouched. My mom and dad have a tendency to turn their kids' bedrooms into home gyms and offices. Jessica's room had become my mom's office/beading/jewelry/crafts room when I was in high school and Kelly's, from the looks of it, was more fitness center than bedroom. When your bedroom has an elliptical, weights, and a bunch of yoga mats rolled up in a corner, your childhood is officially over.

I passed out for a little while until I was called down to dinner. Kelly, who I guess was getting special treatment from my parents, given her recent "exhausting travel," slept through dinner. My mom's Thai lettuce wraps were just as good as I'd remembered. I may have eaten nine of them.

15.

PROMISES

I woke up the morning of Christmas day to an adorable text from Jack. He'd been really good about keeping in touch while we were apart.

Jack 9:32AM Good morning. Hope you're enjoying fam time. Mine seems to have gotten more insane which I thought was impossible. Missing you, babe xoxo

Taylor 9:45AM Hiya:) miss you too. Have a great day today, let's chat later. Gonna go help my mom with xmas festivities etc xoxo

Pepped up by our little text exchange, I showered and threw on some shorts and Jack's sweatshirt before coming downstairs.

The next few hours were spent sitting by the tree, opening presents (I got an iPad and a gift card to Sephora), making dinner and watching *Love Actually* for the four thousandth time. By late afternoon we'd moved into the dining room to set the table.

"So, have you gone overboard with the jazziness level of this spectacular table setting because you're bored and suffering from empty nest syndrome?" I asked my mother as we brought trivets and napkins into the dining room. I must've struck a nerve because she didn't look amused. "Or is it supposed to make Kelly feel special upon her return to the 'real world,' as you and Dad like to call anywhere but Africa?"

"Oh, Taylor, please. I'm so sick of you thinking of me as a racist. I referred to home as the 'real world' once. This is her real world, that . . . where Kelly was . . . that was just very different. That's all I was saying."

"Fine."

"Am I wrong?"

"No, you're not."

Neither of us realized that Kelly was standing in the doorway at the other end of the long, wallpapered room.

"Don't give Mom shit for trying to make me happy, Taylor," Kelly said.

"I'm not giving anyone shit! It was an honest question."

"I feel like you're a bigger bitch since you joined BZ."

We were standing on either side of the table.

"Completely possible," I admitted.

"Okay," my mom said, surveying the table, "this is looking really, really nice. We'll eat at six. I'm going up to wash my face and get dressed. And I'll ask you both now to make sure there aren't any 'shit's or 'bitch'es during dinner, please?"

"Sure," my sister and I said in unison, and my mom was off.

Kelly followed me into the kitchen and grabbed a bottle from the fridge.

"It's creepy how into Christmas she is this year," she said.

"Right? It's not like you just got out of prison or anything."

"It kind of feels like I did."

Kelly poured us each a glass of rosé champagne.

"I think Mom's just lonely as fuck," she said after taking a gulp.

"I think you're right. I told her to make new friends."

"Maybe she should find some friends who do things other than raise money for cancer kids."

I couldn't help but laugh.

"What?"

"We just started planning the benefit for the children's hospital."

"Ewwww, and you're on the committee?"

"Unfortunately," I said. Although I really didn't mind.

"Of course you are. God, they must be eating you up," she said, looking into her wineglass.

"They definitely are. It's weird."

"But you don't hate it?"

"No, I don't hate it."

She finished her glass with another swig. I wondered if she should be drinking so much.

"Alright," I said, refilling my glass and then Kelly's, "I'm gonna try to sleep for an hour before dinner."

"Good luck."

"Thanks, Sis."

By the time I threw myself together and got down for dinner, somewhat dazed by my nap and fifteen minutes late because of it, my mom and sister were chatting over a salad and wine about something Michelle Obama had recently worn.

"Thanks for waiting," I said with a forced smile, pulling out my chair. The same chair I'd sat in since kindergarten.

My dad scowled back. "You're late."

"Sorry, everyone. Attack of the nap monster; he wouldn't let me go."

"I don't know how you sleep so much," said Kelly. "I never want to sleep again. I feel like it's all I did when I was away."

My mom shot her a somewhat concerned glance. I didn't know why, and it was awkward.

"I didn't realize Zambians slept so much. I think of them more as a working culture," I offered.

"Can we talk about something besides me for a second?" Kelly half-moaned as she took a bite of kale caeser salad, a new (and trendy) addition to my mom's holiday spread.

I wasn't gonna let her off that easy. I wanted to know more. "Are you serious?"

"It's all we've talked about!" Kelly said a bit too loudly for the room.

"Okay. First, we have not even talked about it. I feel like I know nothing about your trip, and Mom and Dad told me not to pry because you're tired. And second, I haven't exactly felt open talking to you about all the fun BZ shit I've been doing because you're all weird about me joining and saying I shouldn't trust them and shit—"

"Taylor Bell!" my mom shouted. "No 'shit's! You promised!"

"Fine. Sorry."

"It's fine," my mom continued. "Can we all please take a breather and—"

"No, Mom, let us have this moment. I need to try communicating with my sister here," I shot back. "Kelly. What is going on?"

"I can't with you right now, Tay." She slammed her fork down, making both my father and mother gasp. She looked at their side of the table. "I can't do this anymore."

"You can't do what anymore?" I asked.

Kelly's gaze adjusted toward me but settled near my plate, never making it all the way to my eyes. She stared blankly for a second.

"Okay, so . . ."

"Yeah?"

"I never went to Africa."

Silence. My eyes darted around to everyone in my family. Blank stares.

"Um," I was able to spit out, "what do you mean?"

"I never went to Africa."

"Right. I heard you, I just don't understand what that means, Kelly."

My dad put his utensils politely down on either side of his salad.

"Taylor, sweetie," he said, "we were going to tell you, but

you'd just decided to go to CDU and we didn't want all of this to affect how you felt about where you were headed. Then when you decided to do the sorority thing, none of us expected you would actually want to join . . ."

"I did. I knew she would," interjected my mom.

I was still completely lost. "What is going on here? What does this have to do with me?"

Then I got hit with that sickening feeling of doubt that creeps up when you realize a cop is driving behind you. Even though you're not speeding and there's no pot or alcohol in your car, you're able to convince yourself that you've done something horribly illegal and your mind immediately sends you to prison . . . for life.

Kelly looked me in the eyes.

"Last year, when I graduated and we told everyone that I'd gotten into the program to go to Zambia . . . that was a lie. Teaching the nurses there how to use sonograms and everything, that was all a lie. Straight up."

"Okay . . . uh . . . then . . . what actually happened?" I was doing my best not to raise my voice. My family doesn't do well when children raise voices at dinner tables.

"Well," Kelly took a sip of water, "the short version is that Colette and I were selling Adderall . . . to students . . . lots of it . . . and we got caught."

"Uhh . . ."

"And instead of telling everyone and embarrassing our family, the school, and our chapter, I took the fall and was shipped off to a fucking drug rehab center in New Hampshire that the dean of students picked out."

"No 'fuck's either, please, girls," my mom said quietly, and took another bite of salad.

For the first time in a long time, I was speechless. And only half aware of what was going on. Too much was flying through my head. I couldn't process it all at once. Colette. The girls. Who else knew? Jack? After screaming, "I thought I knew you people!" at all three of them like a crazy woman, I pushed my chair back, stood up, and stormed out of the dining room.

16.

FROZEN-YOGURT MACHINES

*M*y parents were calling for me to sit back down. I ran through the kitchen and onto the screened-in porch. I slammed the screen door behind me and threw myself down on my favorite couch in the house. It's green with lavender-colored embroidered pillows; it's been around since I can remember and was always my nap spot of choice. But today I just sat there, head spinning, at a loss for how to process Kelly's confession.

After a few minutes, I heard someone's footsteps.

"Hey," Kelly said from behind the screen. I didn't feel like making eye contact, so I just kept looking out into the backyard.

"What the fuck, Kelly?"

"It's insane. I know." She came and sat down next to me on the couch.

"I can't deal with Mom and Dad right now, so I hope they're not following you."

"I told them to let me talk to you," she said. "Will you let me talk to you?"

"But, like, what the fuck? What happened? Who knows besides us?"

"Okay . . . I—" she started.

"Why didn't you tell me? I feel like a fucking idiot."

"Stop," she put her arm around me. This was the most affectionate I'd seen my sister since I was in elementary school. "I'm gonna tell you everything right now."

"Okay . . ."

"Just a second." Kelly shot up, went inside, and grabbed two beers from the fridge. My dad drank Corona Lights, which I normally wouldn't drink, but I couldn't refuse anything alcoholic at this juncture.

"I'm just going to tell you exactly what happened," she said, sitting back down next to me.

"And then you're going to tell me why no one wanted me to know. Why you never told me."

"Okay, yes, fine. All of that."

"I don't understand how keeping me in the dark is protecting me—"

"Just let me talk and you can ask questions after, please. It'll be so much easier. And faster . . . I'm actually starving."

I cracked a reluctant smile. My sister is borderline anorexic— for her to admit that she's hungry was a sign of real desperation.

"Okay," I agreed, "start talking."

"Okay. Last year Colette and I were in charge of a campaign to raise money from alumni to upgrade the annual children's hospital event. Colette was a junior, and I was a senior, obviously." She took a gulp of beer. "We realized that we were going to fall way, way, way fucking short of raising the amount we needed to reach the goal we'd set. It actually costs a lot of money to set up the right venue and the honorary guests' travel and all of that shit. And I gotta say, missing the goal was mostly Colette's fault for spending more time blowing Jimmy Ludwig that semester than harassing alumni for cash like she should've been doing, but anyway, that's not the point. We ended up resorting to selling a tiny bit of Adderall that we would buy from a supplier in town to make the money and we reached the goal."

"I thought you said—"

"Okay. Having some extra cash to play with didn't hurt either, so it turned into us selling a lot of Adderall."

"How many people were you selling to?" I almost didn't want to know the answer. The thought struck me—how many people on campus know me as their dealer's little sister? Anyone? Everyone?

"At the end, I think the list was up to about thirty solid customers. All of them in a sorority or a frat. We never strayed," Kelly said plainly.

"Jesus." I knew there were plenty of drugs on campus—I'd only been at school four months and already had my fair share of spiked Red Bull—even sampled cocaine. But I just couldn't picture Kelly as a drug dealer—nor could I picture myself as a drug dealer's sister . . . "Were you using too?"

"Fuck no. Apart from the occasional swig of fun juice, I never touched that shit. Honestly, Tay. Half of that school is on scrips. Especially the srat kids. It's fucking sad. But it's not my fault."

"Um, you definitely weren't helping." There was a surprising anger in my voice.

"We didn't know it would get so huge."

"This is so insane, Kelly."

"I know. I fucking know it's insane."

"So, what does the house know? These are like my only friends at school besides Jonah. How do I . . . ? Like, does Colette hate me because—"

"No, stop. See, this is why I didn't tell you. Let me finish."

"Okay."

We both took sips from our beers.

"So," she continued, "we were eventually able to raise more than enough money for all the shit we were doing. But just before graduation, Colette and I were ratted on by some piece-of-shit ethics major, isn't that ironic, who told a university official about everything. Then, in hopes of avoiding a schoolwide scandal, the administration basically offered us a plea deal. So instead of making it public and crucifying two unlikely drug lords with shiny hair and good tits, they would just handle it internally. The whole hazing scandal at Alpha had just gone down, so I don't think they could handle any more bad press. It was lucky for us, honestly."

"So why were you sent away and Colette got off?"

"Because her hair is shinier and her tits are better."

"Oh my God. How can you make jokes about this right now?"

"What else am I supposed to do at this point?"

I just stared at her blankly.

"Okay. I told you I'd give you the full story; cool your puss. So, we both admitted guilt to the disciplinary committee and they agreed that we would be quietly punished without causing any damage to the reputation of the sorority. Believe it or not, our main concern at the time was that we were gonna get BZ shut down."

"But how could they do that? Why would they do that?"

"You know the bathroom with the green door in the basement of the BZ house?"

"No, I've never been down there."

"Yeah, no one goes down there. We were using it as a storage room for the . . . product."

"God," I blurted, "I'm literally in an episode of *Breaking Bad* right now."

"Aaaand . . . a few other Actives got involved in the selling."

"What?! Who?"

"I'm not allowed to say, but you don't need to worry about that. I explained to them all that they could never mention their involvement to anyone, ever. And if they did, they'd run the risk of being kicked out of school and be the cause of BZ shutting down. No one is saying a word. Trust me."

"Ugh. Okay." I found this hard to believe, but I chose not to question it.

"So, I got screwed by Colette. We agreed to take the fall together, but Colette, who still had a year left at school and more to lose, put the whole thing on me in our final disciplinary committee meetings and convinced the powers that be to let her walk away unscathed."

"What? I don't understand!"

"Before our respective meetings, we agreed on what we would say. We weren't gonna rat out any of the other girls who sold with us and we weren't gonna list names of clients who the school hadn't found with their own investigation. We were just gonna keep our lips as sealed as possible. So I was pretty fucking shocked and appalled and buttsore when I got a call later that afternoon to come back in to meet with the dean and his cronies. Basically Colette told them I framed her."

"And they just took her word for it?"

"I don't think it helped my case that Colette's dad is on the board of trustees. A position he obtained when his fro-yo empire donated millions of dollars and new yogurt machines to all the dining halls. You know how much people love those fucking frozen-yogurt machines."

"What?!" I asked, incredulous.

"Oh, I know. There was so much weird shit going on behind closed doors, I could just smell it. So they allowed me to walk at graduation, you were there so you remember that, but I wasn't allowed to get my diploma until I completed a horrible, *Girl, Interrupted*–type, life-scarring, six-month rehab thing where I had to live with actual addicts and crazy people."

I'd been so hung up on how all of this would affect my life on campus that I didn't even stop to ask her how she managed to survive six months of rehab. I looked down at the beer sweating in my hand, the enormity of my sister's admission finally settling in. "Kelly, I . . ."

"And that's all folks, here we are." She let out a sarcastic laugh.

I looked at Kelly. Her back was straight, her palms pressed against her knees as if she was about to stand up and bolt. I could tell she didn't want to talk about rehab. "Jesus." I was at a loss for the right words. Again.

We sat in silence.

"I just couldn't bring myself to snitch on anyone, even Colette. I didn't want to hurt the house, you know? I guess her priorities skewed a little differently."

"How could she do this to you and live with herself?"

"I've asked myself that question over and over and over. And the answer is always the same. Colette won and I lost. She's a sociopath—textbook narcissist, superficially charming, manipulative, cunning. I was supposed to go to Africa; I didn't make that up entirely. But the internship started in August and obviously I was institutionalized already at that point."

"How did I not see all of this going on? How did Mom and Dad not let it slip?"

"You were a senior in high school last year. You were in your own world, where you should've been. And you were excited about graduating and about CDU. We all decided to just keep it hush-hush. We were trying to look out for you."

I had to stop myself from crying. I was the youngest and they were looking out for me.

"All Colette thinks about is herself," I said. "I mean, I knew I sensed a bitchy, conniving side to her. But Jesus. This? This is insane."

"Honestly, she's probably terrified of you," Kelly said, taking a sip of her beer. "Bottom line: Colette may be a liar who sold me down the river, but she's also a shark. She got off on the business of it all. I think it made her feel powerful. It was weird; we were friends at first and I actually liked her because she was so direct and bossy—you know how she is. But then when it got bigger, and our list of clients started to include some pretty big names on campus, the power went to her head."

As if reading my mind, Kelly put her hand on my leg and continued, "You can't resign and you can't fight her. It will only make more of a mess."

I paused.

"No fucking way," I quietly said. "Of course I can't resign. If I quit now then Colette will totally get off scot-free . . . ugggh-hhhhhh!!"

"Whoa, whoa."

"I could kill her. I knew something was weird. I totally knew something was, like, very, very weird with her."

A tornado of thoughts raced around my head. I was mad and confused; I wondered what Colette knew, or what she thought of me. Why had she let them dirty rush me at all? Did she only draw me in so that she could watch my every move? And who else knew?

"Does she know that I know?" I asked.

"CDU made us sign confidentiality agreements. So I'm guessing she doesn't think you know. And besides, she knows what lengths I've gone to in order to protect Beta Zeta. Telling you the truth would have put all of that at risk."

"I guess . . ."

"Also, Colette is insanely good at reading people. I'm sure she'd be able to tell if you had dirt on her."

"I don't know, Kelly, I think she dirty rushed me because she wanted to keep her enemies close."

"I think you were dirty rushed because Meg and the girls genuinely like you and wanted you to pledge. Of course, the fact that you're a legacy is what made them pursue you in the first place. But it would not have happened without Colette's blessing, and she definitely wanted to keep a close eye on you—of that I'm positive. But there's no way she'd just assume that you know."

"This is so much to deal with . . . Oh my God, does Jack know?" My palms were sweating.

"Alright, slow down. I don't think he knew about it and he was definitely not a client. He's not the kind of kid we were dealing with."

"Are you sure?"

"Yes. Don't worry about that."

"How can I not worry about that?!"

"Jesus! I knew you'd react or whatever, but you are on ten right now when really you should be on seven, maybe eight. It's kind of amaze, though. But, Tay?"

"What?"

"I'm serious about you leaving all of this alone. You need to take this information and just swallow it. Clearly the sisterhood of Beta Zeta and the code of silence among pill poppers have been successful in keeping the scandal—and my involvement in it—a secret. You're making friends and doing your thing and you'll have your own experience at BZ. You can't let this shit from the past ruin anything for you and you cannot get involved. It's not your mess to clean up, and frankly, it's over. Water under the bridge. I fucked up, I served my time and that's it. I can't control Colette and her bullshit. Just don't get involved. You're better than this."

I sensed an awkward smile creeping onto my face. Kelly also smiled. I felt a rush of adrenaline and then boom! It felt like I hit a wall going a hundred miles an hour.

"It's gonna be fine," I said, putting my hand on her shoulder. "I'm gonna go back there and everything's gonna be super fine. Jack, the girls, school. I'll make it work. This will have a happy ending. I won't get involved. It's okay."

"Really?"

"I know you're probably thinking, *let's talk this out, let's make sure Taylor's all good and not gonna freak out later*, but trust me. I'm fine."

"I mean, if you don't want to talk about it anymore, I will not argue with that."

"You fucking bitch!" I said, pushing her back into the sofa by her shoulders. We were laughing like kids.

But it wasn't really fine. I was freaking out inside and I wanted to scream. Most of all I wanted to scream at Colette for putting me in this position and for what she'd done to my sister. Sure, they'd both fucked up royally, but Colette took it to a whole other level of shadiness.

I wanted her to pay . . . but the truth was I'd probably be on the floor of my bedroom later, curled up and not even crying, just thinking really fucking hard.

17.

SHE'S LIKE SMART-STUPID

"*A*re you fucking kidding me?!"

I was letting Jonah have his freakout moment.

"Are you fucking KID-DING-ME-with-this-shit-right-now?"
He was really angry.

"I know. I know."

"Knew that bitch wasn't normal from the moment I met her
at that party at Jack's house."

"Duh, no normal person eats soup for dinner every night of
the week."

I was starting to feel more sane. Jonah got me, he knows me,
he understands how I react to the world. I'd had more than a
week to live with the new info about Colette and Kelly, but I'd

waited until Jonah and I were in his car alone, headed back to school for the Snow Bash (which was supposed to be the most epic Greek party of the year), to drop the bomb. He'd been running around having what he refers to as "forced family fun" during Christmas week and I knew how stressful that kind of stuff was for him, so I'd made the decision to hold off on telling him my interesting news. Also . . . I think I just needed time to try and personally process everything. Not that I was very successful at that.

"The thing that's so fucked up is that this little tidbit of info, like, basically affects every aspect of your life, you know?"

"Like, can I trust anyone at this point? My parents lied to me, my sister lied to me, and my sorority used to run a drug ring." I sighed. "So that's what I've been dealing with for the past ten days."

"I'm sorry, babe. That sucks in a major way."

"Thanks." I stared out the window and realized I'd done nothing but talk about myself.

"Shit, I'm horrible. How was your Christmas and everything?"

"It was fine. My dad's a dick, my mom's a drunk, my brother's an asshole—and his video game obsession scares me. But other than those minor details, it could have been worse."

"Sounds festive."

"It was a festive mess."

"Families are a mess."

"Truth," Jonah agreed with a nod. "I never, ever thought I would say this, but I wish classes started tomorrow. I mean, I'm glad we get to go back to campus, but after the Snow Bash, I have to go back to my parents' dysfunctional home for another week of misery. I could honestly fucking murder you for the fact that you're just gonna stay at school till classes start. My parents would never let me skip out on a week of torture with them."

"Well, after this whole thing happened with Kelly on Christmas Eve, I was pretty much calling the shots in that house. They all felt like shitheads for lying to me."

"Every cloud . . ."

"I guess." I wanted to talk about something else. Anything else. "Will Ryan be in town at least?" Ryan was a guy from our hometown whom Jonah had kind of dated on and off the summer before we left for CDU.

"Maybs," Jonah replied, semi-blushing.

"Well, that should keep you occupied. Maybe you guys could go for a swim together."

"Haha. There's definitely been heavy texting."

"Love that."

"We shall see."

Jonah rolled up his window.

"P.S. I can't believe your preppy-ass sister was a drug dealer."

"No. I honestly can't with that whole aspect of it. Can we move on to a different subject—"

"I'm all for being proactive as a fund-raiser for a cause you believe in, but this is ridiculous."

I guess we had no choice but to keep talking about it.

"Doesn't surprise me one bit that Colette was involved, though," I added.

"Oh, me neith. Nothing would surprise me about that girl. Speaking of little miss drug lord . . . What are you going to say to her when you see her?"

"I don't know. Kelly said not to get involved. And she spent six fucking months in rehab to keep the chapter's secret . . . What do you think I should do? Do I come right out and tell her I know what's up?"

"Fuck yeah, you do. In front of all those bitches. She deserves a public stoning."

"She most definitely does, but it's the other girls I worry about. This whole scandal is going to crush them. They all look up to Colette like some sort of holy benefactor. I don't think they can handle it."

"You're not considering just keeping quiet on this, are you?"

"No . . . I mean, I don't think so."

Jonah pulled off the road and onto the shoulder, slamming on the brakes.

"Taylor Natalie Bell, I'm sorry, but you are honestly brainwashed if you just let this one slide. You and Kelly may not have been that close, but she's your sister, like, your real sister, and Colette fucked with her whole future! I don't know what those girls did to you to make you this way, but trust me it's not a good look."

"Jesus. Okay! I'm gonna do something. Obviously. Retribution will be dealt. But I just need to figure out what my move is."

"It's pretty simple, Tay—"

"It's not as simple as you might think. This scandal is not public knowledge in the house. Some girls might know bits and pieces, but no one knows what really went down. These girls are all innocent."

"So?"

"So . . . they have been really nice to me."

"Who cares? Colette lied to them all. All the more reason to humiliate her and get her out of there."

"If I expose her publicly, it'll create so much tension in the house. And the way these girls gossip, I'm sure it would get out that Beta Zeta was involved in a scandal, which could end up getting our chapter shut down."

"Are you listening to yourself? You're protecting these rando girls above the dignity of yourself and Kelly?"

"Yes, Jonah, I am. Think about the lengths Kelly already went to. She was in rehab for six months, and she doesn't even do drugs. If I go in there now and freak out and scream at Colette, what good will that do? Kelly's commitment to all of them will be wasted."

Jonah just sat there in silence, looking at the road ahead.

"I get it."

"You do?"

"Yeah. I get it."

Jonah zoomed back out onto the highway.

"You have your reasons and I support you," he continued. "But please tell me you are at least working on a plan to privately yet savagely destroy her."

"I might be," I confessed.

"I can help you come up with something good."

"I know you can."

"You have to let her know that you know. That needs to happen stat."

"Really? Why?"

"Because for maximum effect, you need Colette to be squirming every time she's around you, constantly wondering if you're about to blow up her whole spot."

"I like the sound of that. But how do I do that, you know?"

"Just tell her how you got home and finally got to catch up with Kelly. If you say it like you mean it, she'll get it right away. Colette's not a fucking dummy."

"True. But she kind of is. She's like smart-stupid."

"Very, very true."

"I'm just trying to focus on the positive parts of my life. You, Jack, my grades, and my magnificent breasts."

There was no one I'd rather have been with at that moment than Jonah. The rest of the drive we geeked out and listened to the soundtrack of *Wicked*. We sang/screamed our faces off. It was the release I needed after the vacation I'd had (if you can even call it that).

I never, in a million years, would've expected to be thrilled to get back to my dorm room. It was empty and boring and peacefully devoid of anything that made me think of the mess that was my life. I plopped onto the bed and let out a huge scream into my pillow, which was only semi-relieving.

I couldn't stop wondering when I'd see Colette next and how it would go down. I remembered her saying that she was going away on vacation over break, but I didn't know if she was coming back to school early for Snow Bash or not. Until my phone blew up with a group-text string that clued me in:

Meg 3:17PM How the fuck is everyone's break? I'm bored.

Stephanie 3:18PM Same. I'm over being on break. All I've been doing is eating mini muffins

Olivia 3:18PM It's so true.

Olivia 3:19PM A few nights ago she ate like 40 mini muffins and then cried

Meg 3:19PM LOL

Stephanie 3:20PM OLIVIA WTF

Leyla 3:21PM

Meg 3:24PM So who's on campus early? I'm getting in tonight for Snow Bash. What are people wearing?

Taylor 3:25PM I'm here now! Let's hang

Stephanie 3:25PM We're here

Meg 3:25PM Cute!

Leyla 3:25PM Me too!!!

Meg 3:26PM Oh, cool.

Taylor 3:28PM I think I'm wearing this navy halter dress I keep forgetting to wear to date nights

Stephanie 3:28PM I ate 20 mini muffins at the absolute maximum. And they're tiny

Stephanie 3:28PM And I was wasted

Stephanie 3:29PM And my ex from high school was there and he's dating a Victoria's Secret model I'm not even fucking kidding

Meg 3:30PM Okay Steph whatever honestly no one cares

Meg 3:30PM How many muffins you ate

Meg 3:30PM No offense

Stephanie 3:31PM Oh, none taken

Olivia 3:31PM Fuck. I was going to wear a navy halter too :/

Taylor 3:32PM Oh I don't mind if we both have the same color dress 😃 😃

Jane 3:32PM Oh snap!!! TWO NAVY DRESSES?!

Meg 3:33PM omg Jane lolz you're hilarious

Stephanie 3:35PM We should pre-game at our place. Si?

Olivia 3:35PM Don't be a bitch, Jane. I hate matchy girls with a passion. PS who are you?

Jane 3:36PM Oh get off me, Olivia.

Meg 3:36PM Well that sounded a little bit shaaaaadddyyyyy 😂

Jane 3:36PM Me?

Olivia 3:36PM Me?

Jane 3:37PM I'm gonna wear a navy blue halter dress

Meg 3:37PM HAHA

Taylor 3:37PM lol

Meg 3:38PM Colette? Hello?

Meg 3:38PM Has anyone spoken to Colette?

Meg 3:38PM or Kenadie for that matter

Stephanie 3:40PM Nope

Meg 3:40PM Colette, are you there? How long are you in Mexico for?

Jane 3:41PM She doesn't text me.

Leyla 3:41PM Me neither.

Leyla 3:41PM I love when we do these group texts though:)

Olivia 3:42PM I talked to her last night. She's still in Mexico. I think she's in Tulum with her cousins for another like week

Meg 3:42PM Oh ok cool.

Olivia 3:43PM Yeah. She told me she did molly on new years and Lorde performed on the beach

Kenadie 3:43PM OMG fun!!!!!!!!

Meg 3:44PM Oh, hi Kenadie

Olivia 3:44PM Hey Ken

Stephanie 3:44PM Kenadie wtf hiiiiii. Are you here?

Kenadie 3:45PM Yep I'm here let's drink

Stephanie 3:45PM Funnnnn

Taylor 3:45PM PS Kelly says hi and that she misses you guys

Meg 3:46PM OMG hi Kelly!! love love! Tell her we miss her

Leyla 3:46PM Who's Kelly?

Kenadie 3:46PM What's up Kelly. Hi y'all! Let's hang out and get drunk

Olivia 3:46PM You just said that

Meg 3:47PM True

Jane 3:47PM lol

Kenadie 3:50PM lol y'all. I'm so happy to be back

Meg 3:50PM SAME

Meg 3:53PM KK let's talk soon and plan tomorrow night. Taylor call me

Taylor 3:53PM Will do

I put my phone down and looked at myself in the mirror, finding a tense and wired-looking version of myself staring back. I needed to clear my head and disconnect from the world for a minute. I put my phone into airplane mode and got dressed for a run. It was freezing outside, but I didn't care. I knew there was no other way to get out of my head.

When I got back to my room and switched my phone back on to check my messages, I had a voice mail from my parents checking to see that Jonah and I got back to campus all right, and I'd missed this text from Jack:

Jack 5:01PM U back?

I wrote back right away.

Taylor 5:01PM Yup:) when do you get back again?

Jack 5:01PM Getting in at 830. Went to a hockey game with my dad. Dinner later?

Taylor 5:02PM Dinner sounds perfect. Drive safe. Text when you get here

Jack 5:03PM 💋

I'd promised Meg I'd stop by the BZ house to say hi, so I headed there before dinner. I was glad Colette wasn't back in town. I needed more time to figure out exactly how I was going to handle that whole fucked-up sitch.

"I'm running late for my dinner with Jack," I lied to Meg, who was sitting on her bed checking Facebook on her iPhone.

"Oooohhhh. Sounds steamy. I wasn't aware you had moved into the Dicks Before Chicks phase of your romance," Meg replied, not even looking up from her feed.

"It's not even like that."

"No, no. I get it. This happens to us all. You're here for five minutes and you gotta rush out to go see a guy about getting fucked. It's all good, babe. I'm not mad, I'm just real."

"But I'll see you tomorrow to pre-game for the Snow Bash?" I asked.

"It's honestly fine, Tay. I was just giving you a hard time. I have to go in a minute anyway. Jenna brought back some amazing grape-flavored cocaine and I told her I'd sample some with her before we went to the gym."

"How fun!" I said sarcastically.

It was great to see Meg, but it was also a bit weird to be in the house and to have this secret hanging over me. The whole thing made me feel like I'd done something wrong, which was ridiculous considering I was the last to know.

On the walk over to the Omega Sig house, I contemplated whether or not to tell Jack. Something was telling me to keep my mouth shut for now. Did it even make sense to involve him at this point? When I arrived at his house, I stood in front for a minute, trying to find some clarity. As I was about to ring the doorbell, someone behind me whistled.

"Hey, good-lookin', can I help you with something?"

I spun around and saw Jack was already sitting in front of the house in his parked car with the window rolled down. He must have seen me standing there that whole time.

"Holy shit, I'm glad it's you."

"Sorry, Tay. Didn't mean to frighten you."

"What are you doing here all alone in the dark?" I asked as I approached his window.

"I was just about to ask what you were doing standing alone in front of the door, in the dark."

"Good point."

"I got back pretty quickly, unpacked my stuff, and I knew you were coming over soon, so I just came out here to wait for you."

"That was really sweet and semi-creepy of you."

"Also, they're having a porn-a-thon right now on the projector in the living room, so I figured I'd spare you the epic triple-penetration scene that is currently being enjoyed."

"See, maybe you don't know me as well you thought, because I fucking LOVE triple-pen scenes."

"Oh, well then. I am so very sorry to have deprived you. I didn't realize you were such a fan of the adult cinema. By all means, let's go in and see if we can't catch the last couple of moments. Which, by the way, are spectacular in this particular vignette. Some of Tasha Reign's finest work."

"Huge fan of Tasha's."

"She's an artist."

This was the weirdest and sexiest flirting of my life.

"I couldn't agree more with you, Jack. I really couldn't." I leaned into his car window and kissed him.

We made out for a minute, then Jack suggested that we pick up dinner, go back to my dorm, and watch a movie. It was pretty clear that we wouldn't be doing too much eating or watching.

The sex that Jack and I'd had up until now had been great, but after coming back from break it was like we'd graduated to a new level of closeness. There was something new about the way he looked at me and touched me. I could tell that he'd really missed me. Jack was in control of everything. As I laid on my bed, he undressed me so expertly and smoothly that I had a hard time not giggling. I wanted Jack to fuck me so badly. He had a tendency to make me wait for it, which was what I loved most about him. Just as I was about to force him to go inside me he looked deep into my eyes and said:

"I want you on top tonight."

I'd never been on top with Jack, or anyone for that matter.

"Okay."

"I'll do all the work. Just relax," he said.

As I climbed on top and he went inside me, I knew I was going to love this. It felt amazing, like nothing I'd ever experienced. The pressure between our bodies was so intense. I couldn't feel where my body ended and his began. Jack continued to control the motion, but I realized I could control how much I was bearing down on top of him. Within a minute I was already feeling like I could orgasm.

"I feel like I'm gonna come," I blurted out.

"You should then."

I ended up having three orgasms in the span of about twenty minutes. It was incredible and it felt like we were both in shock afterward. I fell asleep, nestled into Jack's shoulder, and I stayed there until the morning.

"Greasy diner breakfast?" Jack asked, one eye open.

"You read my mind."

"Great. I need coffee. Badly."

"I have an extra toothbrush for you."

"Are you saying I have morning breath?"

"Haha, very funny. I just don't trust a man who doesn't value oral hygiene."

"I respect that and I will honor that by accepting your kind dental gift. I shall treasure it always."

"Such chivalry!" I kissed him hard on his perfectly stubbled cheek and he hopped out of bed.

As we went about our morning, brushing our teeth together, getting dressed together, and driving to breakfast, the fact that I hadn't told him a thing about Colette and Kelly was weighing on me. I just kept building it up in my head. How could I be dishonest with someone whom I was expecting to be honest with me? Was I being dishonest by not telling him?

At some point during breakfast, I must have unknowingly started staring at my egg-white omelet.

"Are you okay?" he asked. "You just checked out or something."

That was it. I needed to tell him everything. I wanted him to know what I'd been through. I had to break the seal. But as I looked up, something caught my eye by the front counter.

Holy fucking shit.

It was Colette.

She walked into the diner with this football player named Josh something, whom she fucked from time to time. She looked flawless. My blood started to boil.

"Oh, look who's here," I said to Jack in the calmest tone I could muster.

She spotted us and came right up to the table.

"Nothing like some diner grease and shitty coffee to wash down last night's coital juices."

I'd forgotten how condescending Colette's tone was. Being this close to her literally made me want to throw coffee in her face and stab her with my butter knife.

"Hey, Colette. How are you?" Jack said.

"I'm good. Came back early for the Snow Bash, as I assume you did as well?"

"Yeah, we did." I smiled. "How was Mexico?"

"Hot. How was your break, Taylor?"

This was it. This was my moment. I thought about what Jonah had said about owing it to Kelly and all of my BZ sisters to stand up to Colette. I wanted her to know that I knew everything that had gone down. But I had to proceed with caution; Colette was a crafty bitch and a formidable opponent. I took one long breath, and looked deep into her brown eyes.

"It was really nice, Colette. Finally got a chance to catch up with Kelly. She's been . . . away, as you know."

"Right," Colette replied smugly. "How was her . . . intern-ship?"

"Great! Although she's not nearly as tan as I thought she'd be after all those months in Africa. Anyways, we had soooooo much to talk about—you know, about Beta Zeta and all."

Colette looked into my eyes and, for a split second, I saw her perfectly composed facade crack. Just as quickly, her face resumed its mask of calm condescension as she turned to go. "See you tonight, I guess?"

"Great."

She knew that I knew. As she walked away I sat happily in that booth, convinced that I had played it perfectly. I decided not to tell anyone else, including Jack, about my beef with Colette. Getting back at her would be a long and slow process. Colette had already proved herself to be a masterful manipulator. Kelly is no joke and Colette had managed to take her down. I'd have to be calculated and calm about it.

"Hey, Colette," I called out to her, "sorry about your mom's dog."

"It's fine. Thanks." She sat in a booth on the other side of the diner.

It's on.

18.

THE BZ GIRL

*W*eeks passed without incident between me and Colette. I could tell that she was keeping an eye on me just as much as I was keeping an eye on her—in chapter meetings, in hospital gala committee meetings, at parties. Neither of us said a word about it. It was business as usual on the exterior. Between studying, the chapter stuff, and Jack, exacting revenge on Colette fell lower and lower on my priority list. To be honest, I barely had enough time to blow-dry my hair on most days.

I kept my life pretty much dramaless until one Sunday night about a month or so into the spring semester. It started as a pretty average night. I was in the library robotically rifling through index cards, testing myself on some IDs for a quiz I had the next day. On one side of each card was the name of a feminist visual artist from 1960 to 1970, and on the other were three of her most famous works and a blurb about her contribution to the time period. This was kind of exactly what I liked about school, the routine and the repetition. I was always good at memorizing things.

Completely in the zone, I spat out the IDs more like a computer than a human. *Bridget Riley*, flip card, *Crest 1964, Disturbance 1964, Cataract 1967, geometry suggests movement of color, inspired by hallucinogenic experimentation with Aldous Huxley*, next card.

Ping, ping. My phone buzzed next to my stack of books, causing the whole table to vibrate. The girl across from me, who had been coughing and blowing her nose into the same dirty tissue for the last hour, lifted her head from her laptop and scowled.

"Sorry," I mouthed before reading the text.

Meg 10:44PM House meeting in 15 minutes. Basically if you're not here by 11 then we're locking the door and you can never come back. So don't be late. Not kidding :)

Random house meetings like this were super rare. I threw my bag over my shoulder and got out of that library as quickly and quietly as I could. I knew I'd have to speed-walk to make it across campus in time.

I glanced at my phone as I ran up the faded brick steps to the BZ house.

10:58 PM.

The door was unlocked. I went directly to the Great Room, where meetings were normally held, which was empty besides Jane, who was also looking for everyone.

"Oh," she said, pointing to a note on the mantel. "It says to go to the basement."

I didn't say anything, just followed her downstairs. I'd only been down to the basement once before, to grab some cups for a brunch meeting we had. I found myself peering into every open door, wondering where the bathroom was that my sister and Colette had used as storage for their stash.

Now my entire pledge class was standing around talking. People didn't really seem that apprehensive. Jane and I found open seats in the circle of chairs. Everything these girls did was in a circle.

"This is so annoying. I was showering," Jane said, pissed.

I noticed then that her hair was up in a ponytail, which was popping through the back of a baseball cap, which she never did. It was also dry.

"Uh, thank God you heard the text?" I said unconvinced.

"Okay fine, I was jerking off."

"Really?"

"What? You don't jerk off?"

"I do, I just don't call it that."

"What do you call it?" she asked, giving me a stinkface.

"Um, masturbating . . . ?"

Before Jane could get her next words out, the room went silent. I noticed that Meg and Kenadie were standing with Hailey in the corner by the huge TV they kept down in the basement.

Meg stepped forward, her expression serious as she addressed all twenty-one of us solemnly. "We need to talk, girls."

"Basically, I don't even know where to begin."

After a long pause, Meg looked at Kenadie, who looked right back at her, as if to say *spit it out*. I knew everyone else was thinking the same thing. I definitely was.

"We have a problem, and we also have a lot of questions about this problem. And the reason you're all sitting here right now is because we think at least one of you will be able to help us answer some of them."

Meg wasn't happy. She was making eye contact with a lot of the girls, but not me. That could mean a few things and it wasn't making me any less nervous.

"I think it'll just be easiest," she continued, "if I rip the Band-Aid off and we just tell you . . . slash . . . show you what's going on."

She glanced over to Hailey, who was giving her a thumbs-up. What the fuck is going on?

Meg started walking toward the back of the room, "Alright. I've already seen this and it can't really be unseen so I'm gonna pass on a second serving. Hailey will show you about a minute of it and as soon as it's over, Kenadie and I are going to need someone in this room to either confess immediately or explain what in the name of FUCK this is all about."

She turned the lights off. The room went dark apart from the dim of the idling TV set.

"Enjoy."

Hailey pushed a few buttons on her computer, then her desktop appeared on the TV screen. She double-clicked on a file called "theBZgirl.mp4," and a video box popped up. She hit play.

The video was not great quality, so it was hard at first to tell exactly what I was looking at. I could make out that it was a dorm room that didn't look too different from mine. The same beige color, one painted brick wall, the same window treatments, and cottage-cheese ceilings. The light was dim and the details of the room were blurry. A Mike Jones song played in the background.

Then the camera moved.

Two athletic and familiar-looking guys were sitting on a bed with no sheets on it, and a third guy was sitting in a chair at the wooden desk next to the bed. They were all facing the same direction, yet their faces were blurred. Someone had altered the tape to conceal their identities.

Then a girl walked on screen, wearing only a bra, boxers, ski mask, and what looked like a bright red Halloween wig. I was immediately reminded of Pussy Riot and *Spring Breakers*, obviously. Considering that she just walked into a room full of boys in her underwear, I had a hunch where this was going and I wasn't exactly excited.

It was embarrassing; some of the girls in the room started to laugh uncomfortably. Whoever was holding the camera or iPhone followed the girl as she walked over to the guy sitting down on the bed.

That's when we all saw what was printed on the back of her baby-pink silk boxer shorts: two unmistakable Greek letters—a beta and a zeta. The same shorts we'd each gotten as a gift from our Bigs while we were pledging.

"Oh my God," Jane whispered. The gasps around the room got louder when the ski-masked ingénue dropped to her knees in front of the three drunk guys and proceeded to slide their basketball shorts and khakis off, respectively.

The girl was now giving head to one of the guys on the bed and the rest were all laughing and cheering him on, then she moved on to the next, and the next. Even the cameraman got some. A lot of girls in the room were covering their eyes; I couldn't turn away. I'd actually never watched a sex tape. Not even the Colin Farrell one, and I think Colin Farrell is really hot.

Who is this girl?

Basically, without a face to identify her by, and the fact that the camera was moving around so abruptly, this could have been lots of girls. Based on what I could see, no one in our pledge class looked enough like her that you could tell.

"Pretty fuckin' good for a freshie," one of the guys said loudly and directly into the camera. They all laughed. One of them said, "Fuck yes, my dude! Fuck yes!" Then Hailey stopped the video and the lights were flicked back on. They seemed brighter than when they'd gone off.

"We felt that this would be enough to give you an idea of what this tape is all about, without deeply scarring you for life," Meg said loudly from the corner of the room.

"Luckily," said Kenadie, as she walked toward the center of the group, "we're pretty positive that we've gotten ahold of the only copy of this thing. Y'all don't need to know the details, but when Colette and I got word that this shit was out there, through a source at the gnarly frat responsible for the four dickheads who made this fuckin' thing, we made damn sure it was deleted immediately. After we sent it to ourselves, of course."

"What actually matters," Meg added, "is that someone in this room thought it would be cute to advertise that not only is she an epic gaping hole of a slut, but she's also a proud member of this Beta Zeta pledge class."

"It's literally so disgusting," Kenadie chimed in. "This type of bullshit is not okay, y'all. This is not us. Honestly, I'm embarrassed that I didn't sense this type a behavior in one of y'all before we let y'all's dirty, smelly, basic ass into this chapter. So, here's the deal we're making: until one of y'all decides to come forward as the amateur porn star, you'll all be stayin' in this basement."

"What the fuck?" Jane said loud enough for the room to hear.

Kenadie's eyes darted in her direction.

"Oh, you can leave, Jane. And so can Leyla, Ruthie, Lauren L., Kate, Katie, Lauren S., Katherine, Gillian, Abby, and Emily. The rest of you are stayin'."

Um. What?

"You can go, like, right fucking now," Meg said to the girls whose names had just been listed, who all bounced up and scurried out. Jane mouthed a sincere *What the fuck?* at me before rushing out.

"Those girls don't have the body or boobs to be the dummy in the tape," Kenadie announced. "So instead of assaulting all twenty-one of y'all with a ton of boring questions, and to avoid some sort of a witch-hunt situation, we're just going to wait until one of y'all is woman enough to come clean."

"Have fun!" Meg said as they walked out of the room and upstairs, with Hailey trailing behind them like a baby duckling.

No one was saying anything. We sat there looking at each other silently for I don't even know how long. How was this a good way to solve this problem?

Brie White, who I barely knew, walked over and sat next to me against the wall.

"Hey, um, some of us are wondering why you didn't want to confess?"

"What?" I was shocked.

"It's clearly your body," she said.

"Are you serious, Brie?"

"Yeah, I'm fucking serious. It literally looks like it could be you and I'm over rotting in this basement. My pores are suffering."

"It's not me. But thanks for your concern."

"Are you sure?"

"Yes, Brie. One hundred percent," I shot at her.

"Okay, fine. Sorry for asking. I just thought I'd try to speed this shit up a little bit, but never mind. If you say it's not you, then whatever."

She walked back to her group of friends, who were all looking at me.

Eventually we all started talking. Everyone in the room denied having any involvement in the video. Some girls tried to sleep, but the lights kept me wide awake. Cruel and unusual were the words that kept racing through my mind. Hours passed.

Just as we had all come to our personal edge, the door to the basement flung open. I looked down at my phone; it was 6:30 in the morning.

It was Meg.

"We're gonna let you go because you have class and we don't need people asking us where you are. But, since no one has bucked up yet, consider this the first drop of rain in a shit-hurricane of 'fuck you.' This kind of thing has consequences. BZs may be frisky and we may be good at partying, but one thing we are NOT is stupid. And whoever did this shit is straight-up mentally challenged.

"Newsflash, you stupid dicks: you can never, ever, ever let someone film you or take a picture of you doing something that you wouldn't want your grandmother to see. No one is gonna want to hang out with us if we're in fucking pornos. Jesus. Part of me wants to literally walk around this room and slap every single one of you, one by one. Okay, enjoy your day. Also, go fuck yourselves."

I stood up with my bag and started toward the door.

"That's not you is it?" Meg whispered to me as I passed her.

"No! Of course not."

Did it really look that much like me?

"Okay," she said, "I didn't think so. I don't know what's going on. Text me later."

"'Kay," I said and basically ran out of that house and to my dorm room as fast as I could. I felt filthy from sitting in that basement and wanted nothing more than to shower for the next hour.

It wasn't until after I got back to my room, cleaned up, and turned on my phone that I saw Jonah's text.

Jonah 6:40AM Taylor please tell me this BZ blow job vid on TotalFratMove isn't you. Please please please. People are throwing your name around. Where the fuck are you?

19.

VIRAL

"Goddamnit!"

I must've spoken louder than I'd realized, because as soon as the word left my mouth my roommate, Morgan, sprung up in her bed.

"What?! What's happening?" she shouted, her eyes darting around the room and eventually landing on me and my bed and my phone in my hand.

"Sorry, Morgan. Go back to sleep, it's fine."

"What's going on? What time is it?"

"It's early. I'm fine, go back to sleep," I pulled my sheets up over me.

"No, I'm up," she yawned. "Once I'm up then I'm up."

"Ugh, I'm sorry."

"It's alright, I was gonna go for a run anyways. What's up? You seem intense right now."

This was the most Morgan had ever expressed concern for my well-being—in fact, we'd barely even taken the time to get to know each other all year—but she was the closest in proximity and thank God she was, I needed to unload.

"Okay, I'm gonna give you the abridged version," I said, sitting up in bed.

"Go for it," Morgan replied.

"Last night I was called to the house for an emergency meeting, so I, like, ran my ass across campus like a crazy person and when I got there, they forced us all to sit down in the basement and watch this marginally offensive and one-hundred-percent gross sex tape of this girl in a ski mask and BZ underwear blowing four guys whose faces were blurred out. And now I get a text from Jonah saying that the video was already leaked and people think it's me."

"Was it you?" Morgan asked, straight-faced.

"What?! Are you fucking kidding with that being the first thing you ask me?"

"I just—"

"NO."

"Okay sorry." She felt bad, I could tell.

I reached for my phone to re-read Jonah's text. My iPhone's screen was now filled from top to bottom with notifications from Instagram and Facebook. I scrolled down and the friend requests just kept going and going. I must've had over a hundred.

Oh my God.

Then texts started coming in. A few more from Jonah, one from Kelly, and one from Jack.

Jonah 7:01AM Are you sleeping? You need to wake up

Kelly 7:02AM Tay? I'm getting texts on texts from people about this video

Kelly 7:02AM Where are you? Call me when you get up

Jack 7:02AM Taylor where are you? I called you like 100 times

Jack 7:02AM Have you seen this video?

"What's happening?" Morgan asked. "Your face just went white."

"Um . . ." I mumbled.

"Are you okay?"

No. I wasn't. But I was in such a fog that I couldn't get the words out. I didn't know what to do. It felt like a lucid nightmare.

"Taylor? Hello?" Morgan's voice echoed in my head.

I was stunned to the point of nausea. I ran to the bathroom to vomit, but nothing came out. I just knelt there with my head leaning over the bowl.

Please, please, please. Be a dream.

At some point, Morgan opened the bathroom door and managed to drag me back to my bed. I sat in shock with my computer on my lap. What started as a couple hundred Facebook friend requests in the first few minutes became a barrage of thousands by noon that day. It didn't matter that I wasn't the girl in the video; social media had found me guilty overnight, and there was literally nothing I could do about it. That's how it works. If Twitter and Facebook thought I was the BZ girl, then the world thought I was the BZ girl.

The texts and calls poured in, asking me if the rumors were true. I eventually had to shut off my phone. I didn't go to my quiz, I didn't leave my bed . . . and I responded to Jack.

Taylor 7:23PM It's not me. I swear it's not me

He didn't write back.

It wasn't only on social networks that people were talking about it. The video immediately got national media attention. They weren't using my name, but they were describing me. I don't know who started it, but within an hour of the video's release on TotalFratMove.com I was being continuously linked to it everywhere. By the end of the day, I had interview requests from TMZ, Howard Stern, and Jezebel, none of which I replied to. I had been tagged in more than seventeen thousand Instagram photos, and I was basically Internet famous for something I did not do. No one seemed to care that the accusation was completely wrong.

That afternoon, Jonah came over with four huge bags of chips and sat with me for a few hours while we ate and just stared at my computer screen. Jonah kept saying, "It's gonna be okay, it's gonna be okay," but I knew he didn't really believe it. Fortunately, my close friends believed me. Jonah, Meg, Jane, and the twins all seemed to have my back and were super supportive. My parents didn't seem to get how huge of a deal it was, which honestly was fine—I didn't have the time or energy to involve them.

I made myself leave my dorm room the next day, and it was a nightmare. Everywhere I walked I could tell people were gawking and talking about me. I ran into Steph at the coffee shop and she said she was "convinced it wasn't me, because the girl in the video had thicker thighs than I do," and that it was probably that girl Blair who pushed me at the first Omega Sig party pretending to be a BZ frosh because "she was still angry at our house." She said to stay on guard because the whole thing felt fishy. As I left her, a text came in.

Jack 4:33PM When can you meet me?

Finally.

Taylor 4:33PM Hi. Is everything okay? Did you get my text?

Jack 4:34PM Sorry. Can we meet up?

Taylor 4:34PM Whenever you want. Im not going to classes so you tell me

Jack 4:34PM K. Ill pick you up at your dorm in an hour and we can get some food.

Jack would hear me out. He would believe me. He had to. It was the first feeling of hope I'd experienced in days, but it vanished the second I stepped into his car. Jack was cold and quiet, and he could barely look at me. The drive was almost entirely silent.

We drove to this pizza place on the outskirts of town. I

couldn't help but feel he'd chosen it because we were less likely
to be spotted there by someone we knew.

"I don't know what to think, Tay. I get that it could be someone else," Jack said to me as we sat down at a table in the back,
"but the fact that so many people think it's you is not a good sign."

"What does that mean? That kinda pisses me off," I said, trying to maintain composure.

"I'm just saying, at some point, it's like the truth isn't as powerful as what everyone believes."

I could've puked . . . because he was kind of right. I just sat
there looking across the table at him. Silently. I felt like I was
looking at someone I'd never met and I'm sure he felt the same
way.

"Okay," I finally said breaking the awkward lull, "you should
be here for me right now. I have the fucking local news calling
my parents about a sex scandal that I had absolutely nothing
to do with and you're telling me that you 'don't know what to
think'? What the hell is that?"

"Don't be mad at me, Tay. I didn't make any of this happen."

"You're right, you didn't. But as my boyfriend I'd like to
think that you want to help make it unhappen and 'not knowing
what to think' is not a good starting place."

"I do want to help."

"Then why are you doubting me?"

"I don't doubt you."

"Then what? You're just a pussy? You can't trust me?"

I couldn't believe I called him a pussy, but I wasn't about to
take it back.

"Whoa, dude. Calm down. I do trust you," he said, holding both hands up defensively. "I'm just saying that at this point, I want to support you but I don't know how."

I took a long sip of my water, civilly placed it back in front of me on the table, and stood up, grabbing my bag from the back of the chair.

"Hey, Jack—"

"What are you doing?" Now he seemed concerned.

"You fucking suck right now."

"Come on, babe."

"They were wrong about you. You actually are a frombie."

I left before he could say anything else, texted Jonah, and had him pick me up at a gas station near the restaurant.

The scandal refused to die down the entire week. I was now fully recognized as the "BZ blow job girl." I had to delete every social network from my phone because the notifications never ended. The final blow in my cursed week came when I was called to the BZ house to have a "sit-down" with the one girl I wanted to see least, Colette.

I got her text asking me to come to the house as soon as I could because she thought "we should connect." I was sure she must've been freaking out about how bad this whole thing looked for Beta Zeta, but I wondered if she was also partly happy that I was the one being burned at the stake.

When I got to the house, she was sitting at the counter in the kitchen in front of a salad, decisively moving lettuce around with her fork, deep in thought.

I pulled up the stool next to hers. "Yummy salad?" I asked.

"It's actually inedible. Produce this time of year is a joke."

"It seems like everything this time of year is a joke."

She put her fork down next to the bowl of salad and turned toward me. "I don't want to make this any more uncomfortable than it already is, so I'm going to say what I need to say quick."

"Um, okay."

"This whole thing has become very trashy and very, very messy."

"Yeah, I've noticed—"

"Okay, just let me talk so we can be done sooner."

I wanted to demand answers from her, but I knew better than to do that. Colette was an aggressive animal; if I gave any hint of aggression, she would pounce back. As strong as my distaste for her had become over the past month, she still intimidated me. I hated that. I still didn't know what to say, so I just sat there, obliging.

"We've spent hours and hours examining the video footage and weighing the options."

"I'm sorry, but who is 'we'?" I couldn't help but interrupt.

"Me and the other girls in this chapter whose opinions matter."

Not a suitable answer, but I knew more questioning wouldn't get me anywhere.

"Basically, Taylor, and I'm truly sorry to say this, but the only freshman we believe it could possibly be is you. And obviously, we're not the only ones who think so. It looks exactly like you and you totally have this weird feminist agenda that you brought with you from day one. What we keep coming back to is this idea that not only is it you in the video, but we feel that you may have created this entire thing as a way to bring the chapter down, as a way to hurt us, and as a way to exercise your 'rights as a woman' or a 'sexualized individual,' or whatever you people talk about in feminist lit classes. This is exactly the type of stunt you would pull, and the more I get to know you, the more I agree with them. So, here's what's going to happen now."

My heart sank.

There was a piece of paper facedown on the counter next to Colette. She flipped it over, folded it in half, and handed it to me.

"This is a letter of resignation that we've gone ahead and written out for you so you don't have to go to the trouble to do it yourself."

I held the paper in my hand and felt the blood rush from my head to my feet. Colette just looked at me, almost smiling.

"So whenever you're ready, preferably by tomorrow, we'd like you to come back to the house and make your proper resignation announcement to the rest of the girls. They'll want to know what's going on and I think they deserve to. I'm sure you agree."

"I'm . . . um . . . okay," I muttered under my breath.

She'd done it—she'd steamrolled me the same way she had Kelly. This was all working out exactly as Colette wanted it to. Something wasn't making sense; she knew more than she was saying.

"You can go now. I need to get to Pilates."

I started to push the stool back and stand up. I just wanted to leave. I was close to the edge when I got to the house but this had thrown me over it and I was completely spiraling downward toward the sharp rocks below.

"And, Tay, know that I wanted to support you in this, but the house made this decision together. Also, the board of the children's hospital has been on our ass about resolving this issue. We needed to take action as soon as possible. The scandal is not good for our relationship with them. I didn't want this to get out, but they've threatened to cut ties with our chapter and cancel the gala. We need that partnership. You understand that, don't you?"

I stared at her, then at the salad. I could hear the words coming out of Colette's mouth, and I knew what I wanted to say, but in that moment, I didn't have the power to say much of anything. I was totally out of my body, watching myself from a distance.

"Okay, Colette. You know what's best for Beta Zeta."

"Taking responsibility for your actions is the true sign of a BZ. Thanks for understanding."

"I'll . . . I'll see you later," I said as I walked toward the front door.

I stood on the front steps of the house for a few seconds trying to catch my breath. I thought about Jonah and how right he was in telling me not to join this sorority in the first place. I'd thrown myself into this fire.

I stuffed the resignation letter into my bag without looking at it and just started running as fast as I could. I just ran and ran and when I finally looked up I was standing at the River and it was starting to snow. I kept running along the River toward Frat Row, all the while hoping that Jack would be home. Dinner had been a disaster; I just needed him to hug me right now.

When I arrived at the Omega Sig house, I was freezing. I could see that there were a bunch of guys hanging out watching TV in the living room on the first floor. But the door was locked. It was never locked.

"Hello?!" I yelled as I knocked. I pushed the doorbell frantically but it was broken. "HELLO!! It's Taylor. Is Jack there, please?

"I can see you guys. This really isn't funny. Can you please answer the door? It's fucking freezing out here."

Nothing.

"Haha. Okay, guys."

I could see Dave, who'd come with us on the boat trip, coming down the stairs.

"Dave! It's Taylor! Can you open the door?"

He pretended not to see me.

"What the fuck? Hello?"

I sat down on the steps to the house, took out my phone, and called Jack. He picked up right away.

"Hey." I could tell from the somber tone of his voice that this was not going to be fun.

"Hey, what's up? I'm at your house right now. In front of it, actually," I replied in my best attempt at sounding normal.

"I know. Listen . . ."

Silence. Then a deep breath.

"Jack," I started in, "I need to say I'm sorry for how I acted the other night, but whatever you think is going on, you need to hear me out . . ."

"Taylor. Stop. It doesn't matter."

"What do you mean it doesn't matter? What doesn't matter?"

"I really like you, Tay. And that's why this whole situation is so fucked. You know?"

"No, Jack. I don't know. Can you please tell me what's going on?"

"My house is just coming under too much heat from this. It's like a lot of negative attention right now. This thing has gone viral, Tay. Everyone is saying it's you in that video."

"Yes. I know this. But it's not," I said as tears started streaming down my cheeks.

"It doesn't really matter at this point if it's you or if it isn't. The world thinks that it's you and my brothers just aren't comfortable with us dating at this point."

"I'm sorry, what? Your *brothers* aren't comfortable? Your fucking *brothers*? You think *I'm* comfortable with this whole thing, Jack?"

"I can't be with you anymore. We need to break up. At least for a while, until this thing cools down. I'm sorry."

I could tell from the way Jack was talking that he had been coached. Coming here was a mistake. "You know what, Jack? I think your brothers are right. They definitely know what's best for you, you fucking child. Honestly, I'm mostly disappointed in myself for wasting my time with such a fair-weather, piece-of-shit boyfriend. I thought you'd be bigger than this."

"I told you on our first date how important this house is to me."

"Oh God, suck a dick."

I hung up and sobbed into my hands, no longer caring who saw me. It was all too much. After a while I looked up at the snow coming down on the road. I had to go figure how to save the rest of my life. I stood up and walked back down the path toward my dorm. I heard someone from inside the house yell "SLUT!" as I left.

20.

NORMAL HUMAN BEINGS
DO CRAZY SHIT SOMETIMES

I took out my phone, fighting more tears, and called Jonah.
It rang until I got his voice mail. In a daze I found my way
to Briggs Dining Hall and the next thing I knew I was sitting
at a corner table, mouth-first in an enormous bowl of frozen
yogurt—yogurt that I'd gotten from a machine that was gener-
ously donated to the university by Colette's dear father.

I started to cry. Again.

I was a girl, sitting alone in a college dining hall, eating fro-yo
with Cap'n Crunch topping and crying hysterically. I was officially a real sorority girl. At least for the next twenty-four hours,
until I tendered my resignation.

My phone started to ring. I hoped it was Jonah, but I was

happy to see that it was Kelly. She'd been in New York over the past few days visiting Jessica and interviewing for some jobs. We'd spoken briefly when the video first came out, and I'd told her that I was "fine" and I was "handling it." But now that things had gotten out of control I needed Kelly more than ever.

"Hi," I said quietly.

"Are you crying?" she asked, slightly surprised.

"Yes."

"It's gonna be okay. I mean, it wasn't you," Kelly said calmly and assuredly. "Start from the beginning and tell me everything that has happened over the past three days. Don't skip one offensive detail. And can I just say, I think this whole thing is disgusting and I'm sorry."

I walked Kelly through it all. The basement, the Facebook friend requests, the media, the dirty looks, Colette's letter, Jack, and everything else I could remember.

"I'm sorry, Tay. It sounds like a complete nightmare. We'll find a way to get you out of this."

"I don't think there is a way out of this."

"Stop. You have to think positively. Okay?"

"Okay."

"So Colette wasn't present when Meg and Kenadie first showed everyone the video?"

"No. Why?"

"I'm trying to figure out exactly what's going on here. Just let me ask some questions and then we can get this all straightened out."

"Okay," I replied. Something about Kelly's confident tone

made me feel so much better. For the first time in days, I felt like someone might be able to help me fix this thing.

"So Meg texts you, you go into the house and then to the basement, watch the video, get locked up all night, leave the house, and you never see Colette?"

"Correct."

"That's a little weird."

"What do you mean?"

"I mean, have you ever known Colette to not be involved in something about the house? Last year she'd barely let me send out a chapter email without her proofreading it first. It doesn't strike you as odd that a Beta Zeta sex video comes out and Colette's nowhere to be found?"

"No, you're right. It's definitely weird."

"Something else is going on here, Tay. This is not adding up. Colette just disappears and then reappears with a resignation letter with your name on it?"

"Pretty much, yeah."

"No. This is her. Colette is behind this somehow."

"That's what I'm starting to think. But what am I supposed to do, Kel? She's a kingpin and the video is everywhere."

"Of course it is. Why wouldn't it be? People love this kind of shit. Colette knows that better than anyone. She's pinning this on you, I can just feel it."

"But why? You already paid the dues for last year. Can't she just leave me alone?"

"Well, maybe she's hiding something else. Maybe there's something else going on here that we don't know about."

"Fuck! I don't know what to do." I welled up.

"Just hang tight. Let me think about this some more and I'll call you later."

"Thank you, Kelly."

"You don't need to thank me, babe. I'm probably the reason you're in this mess to begin with."

"Love you."

"Love you too, Tay."

As I hung up the phone it occurred to me that almost everyone in the dining hall was staring at me and whispering to their friends. Maybe I was just used to it by now, or maybe I was slightly relieved from my conversation with Kelly, but I wasn't really bothered.

"Taylor," I heard someone say from behind me. I turned to see that girl Sarah I'd met at orientation. The same girl I'd had coffee with who told me all those crazy/terrifying hazing stories.

"Hi. Oh my God, Sarah. How are you?"

"I'm fine, how are you?"

"I'm okay. I mean, I'm kind of a mess," I said forcing a smile, "It's been a long fucking week."

"You mean 'cause you blew all those guys and they filmed it?"

"That's definitely part of it." I smiled and got up to leave. I didn't feel like dealing with this.

"Fuck 'em."

"Fuck who?"

"All these ASSHOLES," Sarah said loudly, gesturing to a table of bitchy-looking girls who were clearly staring right at us. "They all WISH they could suck that much dick. They're just haters. It's your body and you can do whatever you want with it. Who are they to judge?" she continued, speaking directly to them.

"Sarah. I really appreciate your very modern and nonjudgmental approach to my current predicament. But it's not necessary. It's not me in the video."

"Um, it's not?"

"Swear."

"It really looks like you."

"I guess it does."

"People are saying it's you."

"I know. But it's not."

"Oh, fuck. Really?"

"Swear on my unborn children."

"Oh my God. Ew! Then who is it? I thought you had to be a pledge to get those shorts or something?"

"I don't know. But I need to figure it out, like now. One of the older sisters wants me to admit guilt publicly and then resign because of this whole thing."

"Wow. What are you going to do?"

"I don't know anymore."

"Is it that girl Colette?"

"Yeah, you know her?"

"Not really but I've heard things."

"From who?"

"I'm kinda friends with this girl from your chapter who I sit with in chem lab. Kenadie?"

"I know Kenadie. She said something about Colette?"

"Well, she came to class one morning right after break, still drunk from the night before, and went on and on about what a shitty friend Colette was, and how bossy she can be."

"That sounds about right."

"You know she's still a virgin?"

"Um . . . yeah. Ostensibly."

"What do you mean?"

"Nothing. Don't worry about it. Sarah, thanks so much for coming over here and talking to me like I'm a normal human being." I gathered my coat and my bag.

"You are normal, even if it was you in that video. Normal human beings do crazy shit sometimes. One time I let this guy dress up as SpongeBob SquarePants while we had sex."

"Okay, wow. Yeah, thanks for sharing. And I agree, we're way too judgmental of other people's lives. You seeing me as normal is a big deal right now. I see you as normal too."

"That's like the sweetest thing another girl has ever said to me."

I gave Sarah a hug and started walking toward the door of the dining hall.

"Oh! Taylor!" Sarah called out, running toward me. "Um, if you happen to see Kenadie . . . will you tell her that I should have her money by the end of the week?"

"Okay? Not sure she's going to want to talk to me at this point, but if I see her I'll give her the message."

"Just say it's Sarah from chem."

"What's the money for? If you don't mind me asking."

"For Adderall, obvi."

"I'm sorry, what did you say?"

"Yeah, there are like four of us in class that buy from her. I assumed all you Beta Zeta girls bought from her too."

"Oh . . . no, I didn't know."

"What?! Yeah, her prices are so cheap 'cause supposedly she

orders it in bulk from some online generic prescription sites in Brazil or something? I don't know, I just heard that."

"Oh . . . my . . . God!" It was like I'd been in a dark room and Sarah flipped on the light switch.

"What?"

"Those evil bitches," I said. How had I not seen it until now?

"You okay?" Sarah asked. "What bitches? Kenadie?"

"This makes perfect sense," I said. "Thank you, Sarah. Thank you, thank you, thank you."

A million thoughts were running through my head: BZs were still selling Adderall. Colette must've been dealing this whole time. But she's having Kenadie do all the dirty work this year. Kelly was right, there was something else going on here. Colette freaked out when she realized I knew about last year—she still had something to lose, so she just put my name out there as the girl in the video. This whole time I thought Colette cared about what the school said and thought about her, but I was wrong. It's not about reputation. She's a businesswoman, and I was the one with the power to fuck with everything that she'd built. Holy shit! She wasn't just trying to drag my name through the mud, she was trying to get rid of me.

Jonah had called twice and I texted him to meet me at his dorm room. I was coming over with big news.

I sat on Jonah's bed for a few moments and explained what had happened at the Omega Sig house, and how Jack was the biggest asshole on the planet. Then I went on about what Sarah had told me and what it meant.

Jonah got up and started pacing around the room.

"First of all, fuck Jack. Second of all, they're still selling?"

"Kenadie is Sarah's dealer. Colette has to be involved, because I don't think Kenadie's capable of pulling something like that off on her own, bless her heart. So, yes, that would mean Colette is still definitely in business."

"So, if they get caught she's gonna do the same shit to Kenadie that she did to your sister?"

"Yup. Don't you think?"

Suddenly, Jonah stopped pacing, and turned and looked at me with a funny look on his face.

"So, wait—she knows you know."

"Yeah, what?"

"And she's ruthless . . ."

"Yes, definitely. What?"

"What if she made the video?"

"What?"

"What if she didn't just put your name out there. What if she fucking made it? She could do that, right?"

"Holy shit, Jonah. You're fucking right."

"Yeah," he said, smiling. "You're welcome."

"Holy shit, Colette made the fucking video! That's it! She made it look like me, so she could get me kicked out of the house and maybe even the school. She wants me out."

I let out a huge guttural scream.

"Is that a happy scream or an angry scream?" Jonah asked.

"Both . . . I don't know. I just feel like we're getting closer to the truth."

"Okay, so if Colette made the video, then we need to see her copy of it. We need Colette's computer."

"Give me a sec to think," I said, putting my forehead in my hands.

"Yes. That's it," Jonah yelled. "We get into that computer, we find out who the real girl is and expose them all!"

"So you think I should go public with all this?"

"You have to." Jonah sat there for a second staring at me. "Here's what I'm going to do. I'm going to call Meg and get her to come over here and you're going to tell her the whole thing. Then we will go from there. Good?"

"Great."

"Are you sure, Tay? Once you tell Meg—"

"I'm sure," I said looking right at him. "Let's do this."

"Okay."

21.

UNICORNS, FETTUCCINE ALFREDO, AND A COFFIN

"Heyyy, Meg. It's Jonah . . . I'm fine, thanks . . . Yes, I'm still gay."

He put his hand over the phone. "She sounds drunk," he whispered.

"Anyways, I'm calling because I wanted to see if you could help me with something," I listened as Jonah started to slowly pace around his room.

"Okay," he said to Meg, "you know some major shit has been going down and basically Taylor's getting eaten alive out there. Jack is literally the biggest pussy that ever lived—"

"Jonah!" I screamed. "Just ask her to come over here. Jesus."

"Sorry!" he mouthed back, "Anyway, if you're free, swing

on by my room for a sec. Greenberg Hall, room 344. That'd be awesome."

Her response seemed to be taking a long time and Jonah wasn't saying anything, just mindlessly staring at the wall, then, "Yeah, I have some beers," he said, "okay . . . okay."

"So, she's coming?" I asked, sitting up.

"Yeah, I'm texting Jane now."

Thirty minutes and a shower later, Meg, Jane, Jonah, and I sat in a circle on the floor of Jonah's dorm room like some sort of *Little Rascals* episode. Except one of us, Meg, was drunk. But she was cute drunk, not "Meggy drunk," which is what we call it when Meg drinks vodka. Vodka turns her into a monster. I guess it does that to some people.

I told them everything.

Everything I knew and everything I thought I knew. I told them about Colette and the drugs, and the resignation letter, and what Sarah had said to me in the dining hall about Kenadie, and the money, and my theory about the video, and all of it.

"So . . ." Meg said, "Colette's been holding out on me all year? After everything I do for her? She knows how much I love Adderall."

"Jesus, Meg," laughed Jane. "This is not a joke."

"I don't think she was trying to let anyone in the house know about her business," I told them. She's leading a separate life and she wanted to keep it that way."

"Oh my God, Colette is the devil!" Meg shouted.

"Literally, my first thought. But I just don't get why Taylor is the target here," Jane added.

I caught Jonah's gaze; he was looking right at me. Both of us knew that I'd have to expose Kelly if I was gonna fully explain this. I hadn't thought it through and now I was in desperate need of a good cover-up. Kelly had taken the fall to spare all of her sisters and it'd worked. I couldn't sabotage my sister and let all of her sacrifices be in vain.

Shit.

"It's Jack," Meg said plainly.

"What's Jack?" Jonah asked.

"Of course!" Meg continued.

"What? I'm lost," said Jane.

"Colette is trying to take you down because you were with Jack."

"Meg, what are you saying?" I asked.

"Okay, I've only heard this story from two other semi-reliable sources, so who knows how accurate the details are, but when Colette was a sophomore and Jack was a freshman, Colette allegedly had a huge crush on baby hunk Jack Swanson. Which she drunkenly admitted to him publicly at an Omega Sig party when he was still a pledge and people laughed at her. I know that sounds crazy, but that's Colette. And I don't know if you know this, Taylor, but you're the first girl to pin him down. And with basically no effort."

"Are you serious? Colette liked Jack?" I asked, attempting to sound totally genuine.

"That's the story I've heard," confirmed Meg.

"And when was he a hunk? I thought he was kind of a loser

when he joined?" I remembered sitting with Jack on his dad's boat. "He told me that."

"Okay, first of all, Omega Sig only offers bids to hot guys. Second, Jack Swanson has been a babe since he walked onto this campus three years ago. He told you that he was a loser?"

"Yes." I put my head in my hands. Now I genuinely felt like an idiot.

"Clearly he was just trying to get you to pity slash fuck him with a fake sob story," Jane added.

"They all do that," Meg added, "don't feel bad about it, Tay."

"I can't believe he didn't tell me about this Colette thing, though."

"Probably because it was no big deal to him." Meg took a swig from her beer can. "Jack Swanson was like this cute freshman guy and he was wasted and ended up fucking this other girl that night who was pledging Beta Pi. It was just some little thing, but apparently Colette was completely devastated about being the scorned lover—clearly that had never happened to her before."

"Whatever. He's still a dick," I announced.

"Who knows if he even remembers. He's hot, girls want to fuck him all the time. The only reason I even know this is because when I pledged and I met Colette, and saw how cold she was, I asked some of the seniors if Colette ever cracked or got emotional about anything. And this one sister Jenny, who was from your sister's pledge class, told me that story and said that was the last time anyone had ever seen her fall apart or show emotion about anything. They said it was like seeing a unicorn."

We all laughed.

"So, what's the plan? We need to prove Taylor's innocent. Can we get the original video?" Jonah asked.

"Why do we need the original copy?" Jane shot at him, "We've all seen it, everyone's fuckin' seen it. It's on the Internet, helllooo."

Jonah stood up, "Yeah, no shit, we've all seen it. But there might be more to the video that we haven't seen."

"Like what?" Jane asked.

I stood up and took off Jonah's old swim team hoodie from high school that I'd thrown on before the girls got there. I'd been cold earlier, but now it was getting warm in his room, or I was getting excited, or nervous. I was having a lot of feelings.

"I think it's possible that there is more to the video. There has to be more to the story."

"That's what I thought," Meg said. "It almost seems like the girl was following directions. Ew, it's so creepy."

"Colette is such a whore, you guys!" Jane shouted.

"She's not a whore, she's just a drug dealer protecting her turf," I offered, trying to calm the group. "Colette obviously wants me taken down and she's using the people around her as pawns in her game."

"Like she's done with me for fucking years," Meg interjected. "I'm always the one that has to clean up her messes with guys and other girls in the fucking house because she says I'm good with confrontation. If she wants to walk around swinging her shiny fucking hair in everyone's face and 'giving the best hand job on campus,' then that's fine, but I'm done with all of this bullshit. Taylor, she told me after Christmas break that you were cheating on Jack, and I didn't believe her but I told her I did."

"What?!" I immediately felt the sting. Colette had been hatching a plan for my demise slowly and meticulously since the day I met all of the BZ girls. Maybe even before I got here.

"I'm sorry, Tay."

"No, it's fine. It's not your fault, guys. You guys are all here," I looked at my three friends, rapt with the drama of it all, "because I trust you. I don't trust anyone else right now."

"Whatever you need us to do, I'm down," Jonah said, taking a swig of beer.

"Me too," Jane and Meg said almost in unison.

"Okay, then. Let's head over to the house. I don't think we have much time here. Meg, can we confirm that Colette will not be at the house, but Nancy will?"

I knew Nancy wasn't a threat. She was our house mother, and didn't exactly know or care about the petty house dramas that went down under her "supervision." Meg took a second to think, then quickly sent a text and got a response.

"Yep. She supposedly just got to Steph and Liv's for a pregame situation. She should be out for the night. And duh, Ole Nance is always at the house. Twenty bucks she's in the kitchen eating fettuccine alfredo that she made for herself by herself."

"Poor thing," Jonah spat out.

"Alright then," I said as the girls started to get up and make their way toward the door. "Meg, give your keys to J. If you weren't too drunk to drive yourself here before, which I think you probs were, then you definitely are now. So finish your beers and let's go."

"Go where?" Meg asked as she fished her car keys out of her green mini Longchamp bag.

"To the BZ house," I said.

"Oh . . . right. Remind me why?"

"Jesus, come on," Jane pushed Meg out into the hall and off we went.

"I'm kiddiinngg!!!" laughed Meg as she finished her beer and chucked it into the trash.

"Wait, why do I have to do the boring-as-fuck job?"

Jonah wasn't happy that his accomplice duties involved waiting in a parked car on the side of the house, but we needed someone to have a clear view of the front and back yards, keeping watch on who came in or out.

"Jonah, boys are not allowed into the house unless they are family, and you know this," I told him as he swerved left onto Hilldale Ave.

"So while you guys are in Colette's room trying to 'find Meg's lost necklace' slash search her computer for the video, you want me to just scour the entire basement for the Adderall supply?" Jane sounded apprehensive.

I turned around to face Jane. "There's a bathroom in the far right corner of the basement and the door is painted green. Search every drawer, cupboard, and cranny in that room."

"Why do you think it's in there?" Jane asked.

"Um, I've seen Kenadie going in and out of there randomly."

"Got it."

We slowly crept up to the BZ house and I had Jonah pull

around and park on the corner closer to the side door, in case we needed to rush out of the house.

When we got inside, it felt eerily empty. I was expecting to have to navigate through girls and conversations, but luckily, it seemed like everyone was pre-gaming.

"Hi, Meg. I thought everyone was at the twins' tonight?" I heard Nancy say from behind us.

"Hey, Nancers, we're heading to the twins' place in a sec. Just needed to stop in and grab a necklace Colette borrowed from me. My look won't really come together without it; you understand."

"Of course, darling," Nancy said with a smile, pulling her glass of white wine to her mouth and taking a long sip, still holding the smile and looking at us while she sipped. She was so weird.

We all just kind of looked at each other. I could tell Jane was about to start laughing. I knew we had to get going.

"Well," Nancy finally said, "I don't wanna keep y'all. I'll be in my room if anyone needs a tampon or anything. Just kidding!"

"Ew, Nancy. Please," said a genuinely disturbed Meg as we made our way toward the stairs.

"We all know what's happening and what we're doing, yeah?" I quietly asked them.

"Si, señorita," Jane said. Meg nodded.

"Okay then; Meg and I will be as fast as we possibly can and you should too," I whispered to Jane. "When you find pills, if you find pills, take photos and get the hell out. If anyone sees you down there, say that Meg asked you to find some old party decorations or some shit. I don't know, make something up."

"Gotcha," Jane said and we parted ways.

"Good luck, text me if you need to," I said to her. Meg and I headed upstairs to Colette's room. She lived in the biggest room in the house, obviously. Supposedly it was even bigger than Nancy's. And it was all the way at the end of the long, dimly lit hall.

Her door was closed and locked.

"Fuck."

"It's fine, I have a key, duh," Meg said. "She made me a copy in case of an emergency. When she gave it to me she said that I was her best friend. I believed her but it also made me sad. You know?"

"I don't know, Meg. Just open the door, please."

"Okay, okay."

She put the key in, turned it, and we were in.

The room glowed in a warm yellow tone from the streetlights outside her window. Everything in her room was white or beige or gray. Everything.

"Jesus, why is there no color in here?" I asked as I wandered around her room, trying to take it in.

Meg didn't respond. She was already at Colette's desk, opening the laptop. She was the perfect partner for this mission. She was an engineering major, which meant she spent her days dealing with computers. It was like she went on autopilot as soon as we stepped into that room. For her, this was a test.

I locked the door from the inside, then made my way over to Meg. She was scrolling through files with a search tab open. Despite her drunkenness, Meg was doing it all so fast. It was amazing to watch.

"How do you know what to look for?"

"Oh my God. Okay!" Meg shouted.

"Shhhhhhh. Are you kidding? What?" I whispered.

"Here."

"What?"

"Found it."

"Oh my God."

"Dumb bitch called the file 'sex tape-full,' and put it in a folder called 'PRIVATE.' I thought Colette would be a harder nut to crack."

Suddenly the monitor went black and a play button appeared in the middle of the screen. Meg clicked it. It started the same. There were the guys sitting on the bed, just like I'd seen before, except now their faces weren't blurred out. Oh shit, I knew these guys, they were all Jack's friends and housemates. One of them was Todd Ridgley, who was actually a really nice and funny kid.

"Ooooooh my FUCK!" Meg said in a hissing whisper, "Insaaaaane!! Todd, Teddy, and Nick. Those fucking sluts."

Then the girl in the mask appeared.

"I know, I'm dying too. We need to see if there's more footage at the end. We need to see if it goes on past when Todd comes. Todd comes last, right?" I couldn't remember.

"Yeah, I think so."

Meg sped up the footage, past the blow jobs, until the girl stood up, tackily wiped off her face and mouth with her hand, then, *TING TING*. My phone went off.

Jane 8:49PM Not here. Not anywhere.

"Fuck. Pause this. Pause it!" I said to Meg. The video froze on the girl, her hands rising toward the mask. Holy shit. I had to deal with Jane and I knew what to do immediately, like I was prepared for this to happen. I went to my text list and tapped on Kelly's name.

Taylor 8:51PM Did you ever hide the drugs anywhere else besides the basement?

A bubble popped up within seconds. Thank you, Kelly.

"What the fuck are you doing? Who are you texting? I'm gonna start putting this on the thumb drive," Meg said.

"Shhh, yes, do that! I need to deal with this. Jane can't find anything down there." Then,

Kelly 8:52PM One time I hid some shit in the coffin in the attic

Kelly 8:52PM Look INSIDE the coffin under the cushioning

"Where would there be a coffin in this house?" I asked Meg.

"Duh, you don't remember getting into the coffin at initiation?"

"Oh shit! Wow, of course I do."

"It's in the attic, I think. Are you still texting Jane?"

"Yeah, one sec," I said, looking at my phone and switching back to my conversation with Jane.

Taylor 8:55PM Go into the attic and find the coffin. Look inside the coffin. If you have to break it apart, do it

"Okay, play it," I said, sliding my phone back into my back pocket.

The girl's hands reached the mask, and she slid it off.

Meg gasped loudly, "What the fuck? Kenadie?!"

My eyes stayed glued on the screen. Kenadie smiled and the guys in the room all gave her high-fives. Kenadie started laughing and cheering along with them.

"Nice job, Ken. Baby Jesus would be proud," said an off-screen female voice.

The camera spun to reveal Colette in the corner of the room, wearing a hoodie. A BZ hoodie, in fact.

Redemption.

22.

GUILTY

Meg pulled the drive out of Colette's computer and we got the hell out of her room, locking it behind us. We sped through the hall, past two girls who luckily seemed pretty drunk. Meg offered them an awkward "Hiiiii," but I just kept on moving.

Jane met us outside on the side of the house about five minutes after we got there.

"I found that shit! I have pictures!" she shouted as she ran up to us.

"Yes! Oh my God, okay. We found the video; it was Kenadie. They covered her tattoo," I said, brimming with joy.

We were ten steps out the front door when Colette and Kenadie pulled up in Colette's red Jeep Wrangler.

"Holy shit that was close," I whispered to Meg.

Colette smiled, got out of her car quickly, and beelined for us.

"Oh, hey," she said in her nice voice.

"Hi."

"Um . . . do you need something, Taylor?"

"Nope. We're good."

"But why are you here?"

"Well, Colette, last time I checked, I was still a BZ sister."

"Technically, yes," Kenadie chimed in.

"I was just stopping by to see some friends," I said gesturing to Jane and Meg. "Or is that not allowed anymore?"

"Whatever. It's actually good that you're here," she said, avoiding my question. "I was going to text you but now I guess I don't have to. You need to be here tomorrow morning at ten thirty."

"Um, alright. For what?"

"Full chapter meeting. Every sister has to be there. I think it will be a good opportunity for you to do that thing we discussed."

"Resign . . . from the chapter?"

". . . right."

"It's fine, Colette. They all know what's up. You don't have to talk in code."

"Good. Then I'll be frank. The head of the Panhel will be in attendance, and we expect that you will take full responsibility for your actions, so the rest of us can put this whole mess behind us."

"Totally get it. I want this to be over just as much as you do."

"Well, that's real good to hear," agreed Kenadie in her sickeningly sweet drawl. She actually did look like me if you took away her stupid face, put a wig on her head, and covered up that tattoo. As I walked past them to get back to Jonah's car, Colette touched my arm.

"Taylor. You'll be missed."

It took everything I had not to punch her in the boob. I just smiled, nodded, and kept walking. I had what I needed and there was nothing to be gained by getting into it right now. I had twelve hours to figure out the best way to set the record straight and clear my name.

"Are you going with them, Meg?" Kenadie asked.

"Yes, Ken. I'm still her Big, remember. Regardless of what she did, she's gonna need some support right now."

"Fine."

We said goodbye and walked away.

"Can I just say one thing?" Jane whispered. We all stopped before opening the car doors. "Fuck that bitch," she said a bit too loudly, and we all burst out laughing.

"I literally cannot believe the fucking nerve of that slore," Meg said through her laughter. "We're playing the real video for everyone at that meeting tomorrow."

After taking Jane to her building, Jonah dropped Meg and me off at the coffee shop near my dorm. Meg had sobered up by now and "needed a caramel macchiato to get to sleep."

"Thanks so much for helping me with all of this, Meg. I was kind of losing my mind."

"Babe, it's fine. Are you kidding me? You're my Little, for fuck's sake. I would do anything for you. Colette . . . she's just bad people." I could tell it was settling in for Meg; it was almost as if she was scrolling through past experiences with Colette and cataloging her wrongs. "It's okay, she's going to look like an idiot when we play that whole video in front of everyone tomorrow. It's gonna be Christmas-morning-good."

Meg and I called Hailey to enlist her help with some of tomorrow's logistics. We didn't tell her why it needed to happen, but we gave her clear instructions on how to set up the video properly, and when we wanted it shown. She obliged, obviously. Obliging was Hailey's sole purpose in life.

"This is too exciting. I need a cigarette," Meg said, digging in her bag. "So, how are you?"

"Hanging in there. I'll be relieved when this whole ordeal is over," I said. "How are you? I feel like I haven't seen you in ages."

"I'm cool. I hate my classes, and pretty much everything about being in college, except for chapter stuff."

"Really? Why?"

I realized I didn't even know that much about her. I mean, Meg was my Big, but we never really talked about anything real—it was only house stuff. It hit me that moment that several of the other BZ girls I was friends with didn't know the first real thing about me either. Our conversations solely revolved around chapter shit. This blew my mind, somewhat. But then I got over it super fast.

"I know it's a little late to be coming to this realization, but my major is sucking the soul out of my body. My dad and my mom are engineers, so I guess it runs in the family. But like, I don't know? I kinda fucking hate math and science and engineering and engineers, so it's just like . . ." her voice trailed off into a low hum.

"I get it. Are they like pressuring you to follow in their footsteps or whatever?"

"No. Not really. They were happy I decided to study it, but I don't think they really care about what I do as long as I do something that makes a lot of money or whatever. I'm the oldest of four, so they want me to set a good example for the little ones. Who knows? They're weird."

"Is it strange that I don't know any of this stuff about you?'

"It's not that strange. There's a level of closeness that happens with sisters, but some things never come up. You know? Plus you've been with Jack, which is totally cool, but we would have probably spent more time together if you weren't. I'm just saying."

"Yeah. Well, I'm not with Jack anymore, so I guess I'll be around more often from now on."

"I'm sorry, Tay. I can't believe that dick dumped you. What a cock. I thought he was better than that. I really did."

"Me too. I'm kind of in denial about it."

"I'd be on the fucking warpath if this happened to me."

Wasn't I on the warpath? I mean, I was about to essentially destroy the lives of one, possibly two, girls. I was so focused on clearing my own name that the fact that Jack had basically abandoned me wasn't on the top of my priority list. Now that

I knew the truth about the video, the reality that I was single set in.

"Look at it this way: Colette did you a favor, kinda. If this is the way Jack handles a crisis, then fuck him. You don't want a boyfriend who turns into some pussy-ass bitch-loser pussy-cock when the going gets tough anyways . . ."

"I know. You're right. But it still feels shitty, you know?" My eyes welled up with tears, which annoyed me because I hate crying in public I didn't think Meg would notice. Before I knew it, she had her arms wrapped around me. It felt really good to hug someone.

"I'm sure it does feel shitty. But you're going to be okay. You're going to bounce back from all this and meet some amazing guy who puts Jack-ass to shame. Go home and let yourself cry for as long as you want. You'll feel so much better."

It was late, and I was exhausted from the emotional roller coaster that was my life. Meg walked me back to my room, where I sat on the edge of my bed and cried for ten straight minutes about Jack. She was right. The cry was exactly what I needed. I fell right asleep.

23.

IT'S GOING TO BE SUPER AWKWARD

Walking into the Beta Zeta house the next morning was way more intense than I'd expected. All the sisters were staring at me. I could tell they were all trying to be friendly and not judgey, but it wasn't working. Deep down everyone was convinced it was me. Colette had made sure of that.

As soon as I got into the living room, I spotted Meg in the back talking to Hailey. Meg saw me, smiled, and gave me a thumbs-up; the video was ready to go. *This better work or it's going to be super awkward.*

"Everyone sit down so we can get started!" Colette yelled as she walked in. She was wearing a conservative pencil skirt and a weird blousy top. I was somehow surprised by how thin she was. I guess she was dressing up for the Panhel official, a small portly woman who waddled in behind her.

"I said sit down, please!" Colette yelled even louder. A silence fell over the room.

I think most of the girls knew exactly what was about to happen.

"Okay. This is not an easy meeting to have. We are joined here today by Miss Linda Ritter, faculty president of the Panhel," Colette said in her most serious tone, gesturing to the heavyset woman.

"I've asked Miss Ritter to join us because we need to have a serious discussion about the video that's been going around which prominently features one of our fellow sisters."

I was sitting at the front of the room and I could feel the eyeballs of the rest of the chapter burning a hole in the back of my head. I was borderline nauseated and it felt like all the blood had rushed out of my face.

"Taylor Bell has asked me if she could speak to us all directly about this matter. So please be quiet and give her the floor. Taylor . . ."

I stood up and slowly approached Colette, who mouthed the words *You'll be okay* before leaving me up there, alone, in front of everyone. I reached into my pocket, where I had the folded official confession/resignation that Colette had so kindly written for me. I closed my eyes, took a deep breath, pulled out the confession, and readied myself for this moment. When I opened my eyes, I tried not to make direct eye contact with anyone. I just focused on a pretty vase of flowers in the back of the room.

"Hi, guys. Um . . . Colette asked me to come up here today to talk to you about my involvement in the video."

I could hear the rumblings of the crowd immediately.

"But it's not me."

"Taylor." Colette jumped to her feet and approached me. "What are you doing?" she continued, quietly enough for me to hear her, but no one else. "Just read what I wrote for you, that'll be fine. So just do that."

Meg timed it perfectly, because at that exact moment the television behind me turned on. Colette shifted her focus from me to the TV. She knew what it was immediately. I watched her face turn from anger to shock; behind her I could see the rest of the girls in the room start to whisper to one another.

Meg fast-forwarded through some of the blow jobs, but brought it back to regular speed just in time for the shot of Kenadie pulling off the ski mask. There were audible gasps across the entire room, but they weren't loud enough to drown out Colette's voice in the background of the video, from behind the camera, saying, "Nice job, Ken. Baby Jesus would be proud," and then Kenadie's response: "Fuck you, Colette. Don't take his name in vain."

A few girls, including Leyla, actually screamed. Meg turned off the TV.

"Just so you guys all know," I yelled over the hysteria, "I'm holding in my hand a confession and letter of resignation that Colette wrote for me and asked me to read to you today. But I think it would best, and I hope you all agree, that Colette should be the one resigning from Beta Zeta today."

The room was abuzz. Like, literally on fire. I smiled at Colette and handed her the resignation letter. And as she opened her mouth to say something . . .

"Colette, Taylor, and Kenadie, please come with me into the kitchen," squeaked Miss Ritter. "Now!!"

We were standing in the back of the kitchen beneath all the big pots and pans hanging from hooks. My heart was pounding. Miss Ritter looked shocked, and Kenadie was pale as a corpse and clearly about to pass out. Colette, as usual, looked unfazed.

"Let me explain," Colette said, cool as a cucumber. "It's honestly not what it looks like."

"Well, it looks pretty bad, Colette," Miss Ritter replied.

"Miss Ritter, I understand, and I don't blame you for jumping to a conclusion here," Colette continued, "but this video is not reflective of the kind of sorority we are. This was simply a prank . . . an inside joke gone wrong."

Colette looked happy as she said this, which was confusing to me. Ken looked like she was going to puke. I felt it was best not to say anything.

"How is this a prank?" Miss Ritter asked, now in a harsher tone. "We just watched a pornographic video of Kenadie, wearing a ski mask and Beta Zeta underwear. She sexually engaged with three university students while you cheered her on! Who exactly is being pranked? Am I missing something?"

After a long, heavy breath, Colette looked deep into Miss Ritter's eyes.

"The video was Kenadie's idea."

"What? That's a flat-out lie, Col, and you know it!" Kenadie gasped.

"Shut up, Kenadie. It was an educational tool of sorts: to show the new sisters how easy it is for 'negative press' about the house to get out." Colette continued, "I was against the whole thing in principle, but Ken assured me that she'd be responsible for keeping the video private. I take partial responsibility for letting her go through with this, so for that I am sorry."

"You bitch!" Kenadie screamed.

"Ken, just come clean, babe. It's you in the video, just accept that you are going down for this and then we can all move on."

"GO FUCK YOURSELF, COLETTE! You're lyin' outta your ass. This whole thing was her idea. She told me we had to get Taylor in trouble because she found out about us."

"Found out about what?" asked Miss Ritter, who was clearly confused.

"Nothing!" barked Colette.

"Y'all, Colette is an evil fuckin' mastermind. I'm sick of bein' her damn slave. Tellin' me what to do, tellin' me what to eat. I'm over it!" Kenadie shouted. Her face was bright red and out of nowhere she let out a low growl, lifted her right hand and slapped Colette across the cheek.

The kitchen fell silent.

"You just touched my face. You just touched my FUCKING face. Who do you think you are touching me like that? YOU CAN'T TOUCH ME!" Colette slapped Kenadie back.

I wasn't going to have to say a thing. These two girls were doing fine on their own. Kenadie lunged at Colette, putting her hands around Colette's neck and tackling her to the floor.

"Ladies, ladies, LADIES! Stop it!" Miss Ritter pleaded, as she attempted to pull Kenadie off of Colette. But it was just too wild and too dangerous, so she backed away slowly with a muttered, "You two deserve each other." It was pure mayhem. Colette and Kenadie rolled on the floor. Hair was pulled, faces were scratched, clothing was ripped. Colette screamed: "YOU WHITE TRASH FUCKING IDIOT!"

The chapter heard the commotion and girls started filing into the kitchen to see what was going on. Colette and Kenadie were oblivious to their new audience as they wrestled and thrashed around on the floor. It was mesmerizing to watch Colette come completely unhinged. So much anger. So many screams. Meg and I shared a glance. This was better than anything we could have hoped for.

I needed to end this thing myself, before someone got stabbed or maimed. So I grabbed two of the large pans that were hanging above us and smashed them together. It was way louder than I wanted it to be, but it got the job done. The room fell silent. Both Colette and Kenadie snapped out of their zombies-on-bath salts rage and looked up at me, dazed.

"You can stop now," I said calmly.

Colette stood up. Her hair was a disaster and her skirt had been twisted backward. She collected herself, took a few deep breaths, and said, "This is all your fault."

I was stunned. Even after all of this, the video, the fight, Colette still hadn't figured out that she was fucked.

"No, Colette. It's not Taylor's fault," Meg chimed in from the crowd of girls behind us. "You're a fucking psycho, and you always have been."

"Yeah, Colette. You're a real piece of trash!" yelled Olivia from the back of the group.

Colette had her eyes locked on me, but I could sense that she was breaking. Miss Ritter looked completely stunned.

Kenadie stood up and came over to me. She just gave me a hug and said, "I was a major dick to you. I should have never listened to Colette. I'm sorry." Then she turned and said, "Fuck you, Colette."

"Fuck you, Colette," I heard another girl say from the crowd.

"Fuck you, Colette," someone else chimed in.

It was like nothing I'd ever seen. A chorus of "Fuck you, Colette"s rang throughout the kitchen. As much as I hated this girl, it was hard to watch.

"Even though I barely know you, I hate you so much," Leyla added and I heard a few girls laugh.

"One time you made me leave a party because you told me I didn't have the legs to pull off the shorts I was wearing, and then you slept with the guy I'd brought to the party!" yelled Victoria, a girl I barely knew.

Colette seemed completely unaffected by what was happening to her. Maybe she actually had no heart. No human being could have withstood this type of lashing without flinching.

"Okay," I said, loud enough for everyone to hear, "I think she gets it."

I turned to the group.

"I kind of planned something that I wanted to say to everyone in the room. I've been through a lot with you guys this year. Some of you have stood by me more than others, so I want to thank those of you who have supported me, and tell all of you who were unsure about me that I hope we can still be friends. I mean that. I really, really like being in this house and I don't regret joining Beta Zeta, despite what's gone on over the past few weeks. I want to remain a sister. When I got to school, I thought I knew what it was like inside these big old houses. I thought I knew what it all meant. But I had no idea. Since pledging BZ, I've met some of the funniest, smartest, most insanely clever girls I've ever met in my life. And you all have so much love for each other. Real love. It's, like, weird actually."

Some girls laughed. Everyone in the crowd was smiling. They all seemed rapt in what had totally become my moment.

"I genuinely look up to you guys," I continued, "and I hope you all feel the same way about me. But I'm gonna need Colette to resign if I'm going to stay."

"I'm not fucking resigning," Colette yelled. "This is my senior year! I didn't do anything wrong."

"But you did," Meg said. She stepped out of the crowd and stood next to me. "So if we could do a quick vote about Colette's status, in light of the recent developments, that would be great. All members in favor of Colette's resignation, effective immediately, say 'Aye.'"

I'm pretty sure everyone in that room, including Miss Ritter, said "Aye."

"All opposed?"

"Nay," Colette said quietly.

She said it with a certain sadness. Until that moment, she'd been able to convince herself (and everyone else) that she was still loved and revered by the general population, but now there was no hiding from the truth. She was out. Her eyes filled with tears, and for some reason, so did mine.

"Maybe now would be a good time for you to read the letter, Colette. I retyped it and changed the name to yours."

Colette's gaze drifted to the floor. She looked hollow and empty. The room was silent, except for the sound of her sniffling nose. She was almost crying. I grabbed a paper towel from the kitchen counter and handed it to her. She couldn't look me in the eye.

"Thanks," she said, blowing her nose.

She reached into her back pocket, pulled out the letter and read it.

To All of My Fellow Sisters of Beta Zeta,

In light of my involvement in the recent "video scandal," I, Colette Winter, hereby resign from the Central Delaware University Chapter of the Beta Zeta Sorority. I understand that, as stated in the chapter Constitution, once I resign, it is unlikely that I will ever be readmitted. And only the National Council has the authority to readmit me. I know that I acted inappropriately, and that my actions do not reflect well upon the Beta Zeta family.

The content of the video was highly inappropriate and unacceptable by any standard. No matter how it reached such a mass audience, the video content must not reflect on any sorority woman in general or any fraternal organization throughout the world. All reasonable sisters can agree that this video does not depict in any way the standard or routine of any official sorority.

I apologize for any harm I've done to the sorority at large or to any of its members personally. I know that the easiest thing for everyone will be for me to walk away from sorority life altogether, but it will be the hardest thing I've ever done in my life. Thank you for everything and again I apologize.

Sincerely,

Colette Winter

Colette quietly folded the letter, looked at all of us one more time, and turned around.

"Just kill me, please," I heard her say under her breath before walking out the back door of the kitchen. The rest of the sisters were still stunned. It was like we'd just watched the beheading of Anne Boleyn.

24.

LET'S DO THIS, BITCHES

The fallout for Colette didn't end in the kitchen. She was given a list of required tasks as punishment for the whole sex tape ordeal. First, Miss Ritter assigned her three hundred hours of community service at the city morgue. Kenadie got a hundred. Both girls were asked by the Panhel to officially resign from Beta Zeta. And last—and this was maybe my favorite part of the punishment—they had to make an apology testimonial and submit it to TotalFratMove.com, the site that initially leaked the video. It was unintentionally hilarious and garnered as much attention, if not more, than the sex tape itself.

The apology was basically Colette and Kenadie in full going-out makeup, both of them wearing conservative navy sweaters, talking about how "embarrassed" they were by what they'd done and how "out of character" it was for each of them. After the story broke and the video made the rounds on campus, I started to feel like my name was being cleared. I went from being the gossip item's villain to its hero.

It took a few weeks, but people started coming up to me in the dining hall or in the hallways of my dorm just to say they supported me and that they saw the apology video and it was hilarious. I didn't need Colette and Kenadie to be ruined by the whole thing, but I'll admit that knowing the entire campus was now laughing at them was sweet, sweet revenge. Jonah, Jane, and I laughed harder each time we watched it, which was at least twenty times. There was even a series of Colette memes that circulated college campuses around the country.

The four Omega Sig guys in the video each got one-semester suspensions. I felt bad for them, honestly. I guess they had to be punished in some way, but I don't think any of them knew that they were hurting anyone. I'm sure Colette told them that their faces would be blurred out. I mean, when you really think about it, what guy is going to turn down a blow job?

As far as the Adderall and the evidence we found, I chose to keep that to myself, in the interest of protecting Kelly. Colette's punishment was bad enough even without that. So I felt fine letting it slide. I did, however, flush all of the Adderall down the toilet and texted Jane's picture of the stash to Colette as an insurance policy in case she ever thought about fucking with BZ again.

*   *   *

Before anyone knew it, CDU was covered in blooming flowers and the school year was coming to an end. I had thrown myself so hard into school and friends that spring had totally snuck up on me. We still got to throw the children's hospital gala, and it was amazing. We raised more money then BZ had ever raised in the past.

"Out of ten, what would you give this year?" Jonah asked me, sitting out at a picnic table near his dorm.

"Well, you know," I said taking a sip of iced tea, "I wouldn't change one minute of this year even if I could. So I'd have to give it a ten out of ten."

We both laughed.

"I kinda mean that, though," I added.

"Are you serious? You wouldn't change *anything*?"

"I know. It's been a lot." I let all the ups and downs of the year wash over me. "But even after my sister's lie, the drugs, the video, and how Jack handled it, I learned a lot. Trial by fire. After a freshman year like this one, I'm basically just a more badass version of myself. Am I not?"

"More badass version? Wow, okay, maybe a little conceited? But yes, I'd have to agree."

"Thank you."

"I didn't know you could be any more badass than you were pre-sorority, but I guess I was wrong. I never thought I'd say this, but I love BZ Taylor."

"Wow!" I smiled. "And I know this is cheesy as fuck, but I couldn't have made it through all of this without you. Seriously. So . . ."

I paused for dramatic effect.

"So . . . ?"

"So thank you."

"You're very welcome," he said. "Was that hard to say? You bitch!"

"A little!"

It wasn't really hard to say that, though. I meant it. Having a friend like Jonah, and now having friends like Jane and Meg, was the true lifesaver of my year. People had told me that I was a strong person before, but I wouldn't have made it through this insane year without my friends.

I was getting dressed in my room, Morgan was out at one of her LGBTQ Alliance brunches, and I had Tina Turner's "I Can't Stand the Rain" blasting on my Jambox. It was a super sunny Saturday, which I was thankful for, considering that I knew I'd be outside for most of the day. Some of the BZ girls were taking me skydiving. Not exactly something I ever thought I'd want to do, and I wasn't exactly sure that I wanted to even now, but I was going with it. I'd been through a lot with these girls, and jumping out of a plane while screaming at the top of my lungs seemed like a pretty perfect way to round out the year of craziness.

I threw my hair into a high pony and was out the door with my bag. When I got outside, I noticed a familiar pair of worn-in Sperry Top-Siders sticking out of a bush near the entrance to Lincoln Hall. Attached to the feet in the boat shoes, literally lying in the bushes, was a very hungover, very bloated, and very depressed-looking Jack. It was the worst I'd ever seen him look. We hadn't seen each other in weeks, but I had no idea that he had let himself go this . . . far.

"Tay!" he half-shouted as he stumbled up from where he was sitting on the ground. I guess he'd been sleeping there waiting for me to come out?

"Hi," I said, probably making a what-are-you-doing-here face. He rocked on his feet until he found his balance. Clearly Jack wasn't only hungover, he was still wasted from the night before.

"We need to talk. We need to be talking. I texted you," he slurred.

Per Jane's suggestion, I'd had his number blocked from my phone.

"Oh, you did? Weird. I didn't get any." I didn't want to be a bitch to him, and it wasn't like I enjoyed seeing him in pain. But I was still hurt and I wasn't just gonna fall for a drunken attempt at connection after weeks of nothing.

After the scandal and even after Colette and Kenadie's confession video, he never reached out to me, never apologized for being a dick, nothing. And now here he was drunk, alone, and a little bit fatter on the steps of Lincoln Hall. It was all too little, too late.

"Can I?" he said, opening his arms out wide. There were stains coming through the cotton under the armpits of his dirty yellow Polo shirt. "Can I?"

"Can you what?"

"Can I just give you a hug, Tay?"

He threw his arms around me. Despite him smelling like a
night of beer and cigarettes (he didn't used to smoke), hugging
Jack felt kind of good. For a second. Then I remembered who I
was hugging and my nostalgia for when we were happy together
faded quickly. I could see over his shoulder that Jane's car had
pulled up to the curb and she was waving at me from the driver's
seat with a puzzled and slightly concerned look on her face. I
held up a "one second" finger.

"Jack," I said pulling away, "I'm not sure what you're doing
here, but I'm on my way out and I really gotta go."

"Okay, okay. I just . . . I feel like you and me should try to
work it out."

"Work what out?"

"Work us out. Us being together. Like, we all make mistakes,
I get it."

"I'm sorry. Maybe I'm not following. You get what?" I was
starting to be annoyed.

"I mean, I'm just saying that we should be together."

God, he was a mess. Was he always such a mess? Had I just
been too smitten and surprised that a big-shot popular dude like
Jack was into me to see this side of him? No, he'd definitely let
himself go since we broke up.

"Well, Jack. I hate to say it, but I really just don't agree with
you."

"Um, okay . . . ?"

"Because, and I may not know everything about how to keep
a relationship healthy, but I do know that a boyfriend should
trust his girlfriend and not jump on shitty gossip bandwagons
just because his loser frat brothers tell him to do so."

"This isn't about my house, or the guys . . ."

"And I have too much respect for myself to be with someone like that."

"Taylor," he put his hand on my shoulder and I calmly removed it.

"So enjoy your day, Jack. I have to run. Oh, and take a shower. You smell homeless and you look like an alcoholic Republican dad."

I turned and started walking toward Jane's car before he could say anything. I didn't look back. When I got in, Jane just looked at me.

"He was sleeping in a bush when I got downstairs. I have no idea. He's an idiot."

"Um, what?" Jane started laughing.

"I know."

She turned the key in the ignition and we sped off.

"What did he say? Why did you hug him?"

"He hugged me! Ew, I would not hug him voluntarily. And you know what? He didn't even say sorry. Not once."

"Has he ever said sorry? For any of it? For being such a fuck-face?"

"Nope," I said, looking out at the passing row of sororities.

It was true. Through all of this, Jack had never once apologized for the way he'd handled himself.

Jane and I didn't say anything for a few blocks. Eventually, she broke it.

"He looked so fat."

We both broke into hysterical laughter. I mean, it was sad to see him that way, but not that sad. Jack had dug his own grave, and I knew that driving away from him in a car with one of my new best friends was exactly where I needed to be.

We pulled up to the little airport in Churchville at around 11:00, and immediately I saw Meg, the twins, and a few other girls standing around taking selfies.

"Let's do this, bitches," Meg said as we walked up to them. I was nervous but pretending not to be. A few cute Australian guys taught our training class and showed us how to strap into all the gear. We would each be jumping out of the plane strapped to one of these hot guys, which I was not opposed to. I could tell that Jane was more interested in talking to them than putting on her vest correctly. Her capacity to lure men in any and all situations was amazing to me. Watching her banter with the Australians was actually a good distraction from my nerves.

We all piled into the little plane and up we went.

"Is this a bad idea?" Olivia said to the group of us as we started to reach "diving height" and the plane leveled out. Her eyes were huge and I could tell she was basically dying inside.

"Of course," Meg shouted back, "but would it be fun if it was a *good* idea?"

"You make a good point, Biggles," I shouted to Meg, who was sitting right across from me. She smiled and blew me a kiss.

"Love you, my brave little nugget," she said to me.

"Love you too," I said, blowing a kiss back.

Seated closest to the hatch, Meg and her partner, Greg,

were the first to jump. Then it would be me, and so on. We all screamed when they started getting set up to go, half out of fear and half because we were running on pure adrenaline. I never thought I'd do this, but here we were. Together.

"Fuck YESSSSS!" Meg screamed, toes hanging over on the ledge. "Fuck yes BZ!!!!! Wooooo!!! We shall steadfastly—"

They jumped out. I could hear her screaming for about a nanosecond before it faded into the windy, bright day. Okay, I was next. I figured if Meg could do it, then so could I. I really did love Meg like my own sister, which was funny for me. I came into this year with one idea of who I was and who my "people" were, and now it was ending and I was surrounded by girls I never could've imagined being this close to. It had been maybe the best and worst year of my life. I would've never met these girls and partied with them and laughed with them if I hadn't decided to take the risk and just jump in. What if I had *never joined BZ*? What if I'd *never jumped*?

"Taylor?" I heard a voice from behind me say. It was Sam, the six-foot man strapped to my back. I hadn't even realized it, but we were now looking out into the sky. It was so blue and beautiful.

"I'm gonna count to three and on the sound of 'three' you and I are both going to simply rock forward and let the wind take us. Deal?"

I didn't say anything. I just stared out at the sky. Not down, but out. I wasn't scared anymore.

"Taylor?" he said, louder this time.

"Yep, I'm ready!" I shouted. A big grin on my face.

"Alright, buddy. Here we go."

I could hear the girls cheering behind me.

One . . .

Two . . .

Three.

Acknowledgments

First, I have to thank my family: Mom, Dad, Kelly, and Jess. You guys mean everything to me. Next I have to thank my "other family": Jonah Brown, Meg Landry, Jane Brandt, Olivia Broeder, Stephanie Broeder, Sarah Stevenson, and the rest of my girls—you know who you are and you know how much I love you. Okay, now that that's out of the way . . .

There's no way in hell this book would've been possible without the help of the amazing team behind me. I'd like to thank Tanner Cohen and David Oliver Cohen (without them, there never would've been a book called *Dirty Rush*), Rebecca Martinson, Byrd Leavell (my super-amazing agent who believed in me and my story), Tricia Boczkowski (the best editor on planet Earth) and everyone at Gallery/Simon & Schuster, Madison Wickham, Ryan Young, W. R. Bolen, Veronica Ruckh, Catie Warren and the Total Frat Move and Total Sorority Move families, Lara Schoenhals, Jason Richman, Howie Sanders, David Ludwig, Paige Cohen, Cristi Andrews Cohen, Penelope Ziggy Cohen, Hal Winter Cohen, Marcia Cohen, Stewart Cohen, Jessica Lindsey, Natalie Stevenson-Cohen, Luce Amelia Stevenson-Cohen, Babe Walker, Stephanie Krasnoff, Olivia Wolfe, Kristina Creighton, and Liz and Frank Newman.

And a big shout-out to Colette's mom's dead dog.